ISBN: 979-8-9859829-3-0

Book/Cover Design by: **MATT DURAND**

From The Ruins

—

MATT DURAND

Chapter 1

I see a dead bird, a robin, I think, sprawled out on the sidewalk. I'm late, but seeing the bird there, so still, so peaceful, causes me to pause. I wonder how it died as I stare at the stiff black wings and orange chest. Had I the time, I would've gotten it off the street to give it the dignity of a proper burial in a trash can at least. But time's not on my side. The increase in checkpoints and blockades makes it difficult to get around. I can hear my wife's voice telling me I should've left sooner, and she would be right, of course. I should've known better. She's always trying to help, but sometimes I can't seem to get out of my own way.

I round a corner and cross the street. Five blocks to go; the rest of the way is a straight shot. Last month I would've covered the same distance in under ten minutes. Now, it's anybody's guess. Everything bristles like an electrical wire on the brink of combustion. The city, known as D.C. Two, is on edge. Two decades ago, the back of America bent to the point of breaking. So the powers that be came up with the idea to build a new city in a patch of woodlands to the southeast of Washington, D.C., where the Potomac River meets the Chesapeake Bay. The plan was to create a place where a mixture of different ideas could come together to form a new model of what America could be. It was a symbolic fresh start for the country to keep it unified. Similar to a married couple having a kid to stave off divorce. The city's grandeur would be greater than New York City's, designed with the latest technological advances. Both sides, the Left and the Right, begrudgingly agreed for the sake of jobs and giving the economy a boost. Once construction of the city finished, however, they had to come up with what to call it, and both sides reverted to disagreeing. In the end, they kept the name that came with the original proposal for the idea. D.C. Two.

I check my watch. I'm ten minutes late. If I hit the twenty-minute mark, my wife will go into the appointment on her own. I would never hear the end of it. If it were any other appointment, I could smooth it over without too much personal cost, but this one is a big one. I need to focus. I take long strides—one block down, then another. I pass the florist shop and stop. I recheck my watch and do a quick breakdown of my remaining time. Eight minutes left until the twenty mark. That leaves me two minutes for flowers—orange roses, her favorite— giving me six minutes to devour three blocks. I peek through the shop window and see no one inside. It can be done. The flowers, I reason, will buy me an extra five minutes anyway.

I burst into the shop and hustle to the tall glass refrigerators. I snatch the bouquet, spin from the door like I'm a running back dodging a linebacker, and spike the flowers at the register. May is behind the counter. She glances at me through her thick purple framed glasses. With her forearm, May brushes a strand of wiry gray hair out of her face. She puts down a pair of pruning shears and wipes her hands on her green striped apron.

"What jam are you trying to get out of this time?" she says.

"What makes you think I'm in one?"

"Thirty years on the job."

"I'm late for an appointment."

"Twenty bucks," she says. "You think this will get you off the hook?"

I tap my phone on the register scanner. "No, but it'll stave off my execution."

May releases a raspy smoker's cough as she hands me the flowers.

"Good luck, Romeo."

I put two dollars in her tip jar before taking the bouquet.

"I'll need it," I say as I'm halfway out the door. "Stay safe."

I sprint down the next block, dodging cars as I cross the street. At the end of the last block, I notice a black SUV parked half on the sidewalk. I slow my pace as I see three soldiers from the Left grappling with a guy in an alcove of an apartment building. The guy they're scuffling with is heavy set, wearing jeans, military boots, and a red t-shirt with a matching red trucker hat. One of the soldiers smacks the trucker hat off of the guy while another soldier tries restraining him. The guy curses at them, flailing one free arm at the other two soldiers. A couple of onlookers are filming the whole scene unfolding. The third soldier pulls out a two-foot metal rod. It's a taser but on steroids, or so I'm told. The insurgents on the Right nicknamed it the 'Piss Stick' since it sends enough electricity into a person to cause them to piss their pants. The third soldier swings it low, catching the guy on the side of his knee. The guy buckles and yells out before the rod lands in his gut. A crackle of electricity flows from the rod into the guy's stomach. He screams in agony as his body spasms with unnatural violence, then crumples to the ground, taking one of the soldiers with him. I keep my head down as the soldiers heave the guy into the trunk of the SUV. The third soldier makes eye contact with me as I pass by. He grins before he gets into the driver's seat. I don't look back as I navigate the final street.

Outside the building, I stop to collect myself. I glance at the flowers and see a wilted rose amongst the batch. I hadn't noticed it at the florist. The petals are black and purplish like a bruise. I brush aside its siblings and extract the lone flower. A small section of landscaping sits to the right of the steps. With two fingers, I dig out a shallow trench beneath a shrub, place the flower in, and then swipe the soil on top with my palm. The hands-on my watch wave at me. I'm twenty-two minutes late. I fling the door open, bypass the elevator, and scale the stairs three at a time. I emerge into a long hallway, following it until I reach the doctor's office.

Inside, a middle-aged receptionist smiles as I scan the waiting room for my wife. My stomach sinks when I don't see her.

"Can I help you?" the receptionist says.

"Hi, my name is Ezra Asher. My wife is Isla. She has an appointment at four. I'm sorry I'm late."

The receptionist types while she studies her computer monitor.

"Yes, your wife checked in. She's with the doctor now. Come around, and I'll bring you down."

I move to the side door and wait for the receptionist to let me in.

"This way," she says.

As I'm following, I lean near her and say, "Could you tell how mad she was?"

The receptionist scrunches her face, confused.

"What?"

"Nevermind."

She stops at the door and gently knocks, and without waiting for a response, she cracks the door open to let me through. The room is bright and clean. My wife lays on the exam table with her black hair resting loosely down to her shoulder. She's wearing leggings and a loose blouse with black dots on it. The doctor sits in a swivel chair next to her.

"I'm sorry I'm late," I say.

My wife doesn't look at me as I come to her side and kiss her on the cheek. When the doctor avoids my eyes, I know something's wrong.

"Mr. Asher, I'm glad you could join us," Dr. Khatri says. "As I just explained to your wife, the ultrasound showed the growth of the fetus isn't where it should be based on the week that your wife is at. And I'm afraid the faint heartbeat confirmed things for me."

"What are you saying?" I ask, despite already knowing what she's implying.

"Well, unfortunately, I don't see this pregnancy coming to term."

"Oh," I mumble as her words register. "I see."

I turn to my wife. She still won't look at me, but she lets me hold her hand. I can feel her anger and disappointment through the pressure of her grip.

"I know this isn't the news you both were looking to hear," Dr. Khatri says as she scrolls through some files on her computer. "Even though this is your third miscarriage, I don't want you to get discouraged. I wish things were straightforward with creating life, but sometimes this is the way it goes. I'd recommend we do the same procedure as last time to remove the fetus."

My wife nods.

Doctor Khatri continues, "Ok, so once we do that, I would say to try again in about three months. If we find that things still aren't sticking, then we can consider some alternate options. You're able to get pregnant, though. That's always a good sign. These things are never easy, but there's still hope."

She turns back to us and says, "Do either of you have questions?"

My wife and I shake our heads that we don't.

"All right then, you can schedule the procedure with reception, and I'll see you soon."

Dr. Khatri stands and gives my wife a reassuring caress on her shoulder.

"Hang in there," she says. She smiles at me, then leaves.

Isla slides off the exam table, wiping the excess jelly off her flat stomach with a wad of tissues.

"Do you want to talk about it?" I ask her.

"What's there to talk about?" she says. "My womb's a dusty wasteland."

"I think that's a little extreme."

She sighs and finally turns to look at me. "I'm sorry."

"You don't have anything to apologize for, ever."

Before hugging her, I wipe the tears from the corners of her eyes with my thumb. I breathe her in, smelling the faint familiar scents of lemon and honey.

"Let's get out of here," I say.

"Aren't you forgetting something?" Isla says, nodding at the flowers, then taps her watch. "Twenty-two minutes late."

I smile as I hand her the bouquet.

"Will I be forgiven?"

"You're lucky you're so damn lovable," she nudges me in the ribs as she admires the orange petals. "They're lovely."

We ride the elevator in silence and walk out into the noise of the city. We stroll arm in arm towards home.

"Do you think we should stop trying?" she asks.

"Is that what you want?"

She shrugs, "No, I guess not. I just thought this was going to be the one, you know? Khatri says there's nothing wrong with either of us, but it's tough to believe her sometimes."

"It'll happen eventually."

"Yeah, maybe. I'm not getting any younger, though."

"She said stress can play a factor too, don't forget."

"I know."

The sun dips behind a building casting us in shadows. People are thinning from the streets as the curfew gets closer. The familiar unrest between the two sides boiled over about a year ago. Ten pressure cooker bombs packed inside the back of a delivery truck decimated a government building after the Left won an election that shifted the power dynamic heavily in their favor. Violent acts started happening almost every month following the bombing. As time wore on, it became apparent that an all-out war was coming. Each side saw D.C. Two as the prize. Whoever controlled it would have an advantage in the battles that would surely follow. To curb some of the violence and hold onto their majority, the Left put in checkpoints and curfews, which only served to anger the Right further. Many people fled, but where to go is getting more challenging as the unrest takes hold across every city in the country. Each day brings the potential for chaos.

I draw Isla nearer. I wish I could pull her inside of me and absorb all of the hurt. But I can't, so I ask, "How does Mexican, a massage, and binging trashy reality shows sound?"

"I have been dying for a margarita." She squeezes my arm a little tighter and looks at me with her walnut-colored eyes and smooth tan face that's perfectly proportioned. A face I never get tired of gazing at.

"I love you," she says.

"I love you too."

"And we're definitely ordering a pitcher of margaritas."

"Ask and you shall receive."

We head a block east toward the restaurant. I take out my phone to order our food.

"You want the usual?" I say.

"Yeah."

I put the order in; then, we continue walking in silence. We've been here before with miscarriages. The first time was tough, but it was more challenging the second time. One miscarriage we took as a relatively normal thing. Two, though, and now three, meant we might have to accept the idea of never having children. Something we both wanted for a long time. A family of our own. Part of what drew us together was our shared messed-up and tragic family dynamics. Death, abandonment, mental illness, and alcohol were terms used to describe our upbringings. By the time we were in our twenties, our family structure was nonexistent. Starting a family of our own and doing it better than what we were afforded always appealed to us. We never thought it would be something we would struggle with achieving. You have sex, and boom, you've got a kid. That was the expectation I had going into it anyway. I guess that was a naive way of thinking.

Isla laughs to herself.

"What?" I ask.

"One of my students today told me about her mom having another baby over the weekend. They named her Naomi. And I thought that's a pretty name. I added that to the list of candidate names if we had a girl. Suppose that was preemptive. I probably jinxed it by thinking that."

"That is a nice name," I say, trying to mask the morose tinge in my voice.

"Well, let's talk about something else," she says, wrapping herself tighter around my arm. "How was your day?"

"Busy. It seems like the Right is going out of their way to damage the power grids."

"I don't get why we don't just let them break off and do their own thing. If they want to be their own country, then go for it. Good riddance. It's not worth the headache anymore."

"Yeah, true. I think it's more about what it represents. If the country divides, it's like we failed."

"I think we've already failed, but no one wants to come out and say it."

We reach the restaurant. A few customers fill the inside, and a guy who looks like he hasn't slept in days greets us. I show him my phone for our order. He heads to the kitchen and returns a minute later with two bags.

"How is it out there?" he asks.

"Quiet right now," I say.

"Let's hope it stays that way," he frowns. "Have a good night."

We wave and head back into the city that, as the sun sets,

feels more like a prehistoric cave filled with creatures of the night ready to devour us whole.

Chapter 2

WEEK 1 - SEPTEMBER 20

I wake to Isla's voice as my alarm. It's six in the morning, and she's still sleeping. Her sultry voice tells me it's time to rise and shine and have a beautiful day. I had her record it for me when we were on our honeymoon as a joke, but then I ended up liking it and have used it ever since. I get up and do a short circuit of pushups, crunches, and stretching. Then I go to the kitchen and hand grind some coffee. While the water boils in the electric kettle, I head to the bathroom for my daily shaving ritual. My dad taught me the technique when I was fourteen. It's the one memory I choose to keep of him. I shave and then take a three minute cold shower. I towel off, slip on my boxers and a t-shirt, then slide into my work uniform, a charcoal gray one-piece coverall with patches of orange on the elbows and knees. The water comes to a boil when I get back into the kitchen. Rich scents of earth and dark chocolate hit my nose as the steaming water covers the grounds in the French press.

While the coffee rests, I scramble four eggs with cheese, butter some lightly browned toast, and wash a bowl of blueberries. I make two plates, pour the coffee into a mug, then fill two thermoses with the rest. I devour my breakfast in minutes. On a small oak tray, I place the other plate and cup of coffee. Isla stirs as I set the tray on her nightstand.

"That godforsaken alarm has got to go," she mumbles.

"Don't you speak about my wife like that."

"When will you be home?"

"I'm not sure yet. I'll text you with updates."

"Come back to me in one piece."

"Always," I say as I bend to kiss her gently on the lips. "Have a good day."

In the kitchen, I grab my keys and unlock a drawer next to the fridge. Inside is my Leatherman MUT EOD multitool, metal pen light, waterproof lighter, and Victorinox watch with a paracord strap. Since the weapons ban went into effect, this has been my kit. The knife on the multitool could get me in trouble, but I take the risk. The Left is more concerned about guns or anything heavy hitting. I toss the items into my pockets, grab the coffees, and I'm out of the apartment.

On the street, I spot my ride, a utility truck with matching brand colors of orange and gray. Plastered on the side of the truck is the company name Helios Solar. My best friend and coworker, Cooper Danvers, sits behind the wheel. He's scratching a spot behind his ear as I open the door. He smiles his signature smile. Not a movie star smile, but a brawler's smile. He's missing a tooth to the right of his left incisor. It got knocked out at an intramural rugby game during a dust-up. His wife thought it made him look rugged, so he never got it fixed. I hand him a coffee. He takes a sip from the stainless steel mug and then puts it in a cup holder.

"How goes it?" he says.

"Good, man. Where are we off to today?"

"Sector five."

"Routine or battle damage?"

"Battle damage from the sounds of it. Targeted another solar field. Guess the Righties have got RPGs now. Deakins told me soldiers secured the site, so now we can get in there and do our thing."

"Damn, when did they get RPGs?"

"Beats me."

"Things are going off the rails."

"We're dealing with people that aren't operating in the same plane of reality. So none of this is surprising. It was only a matter of time before something like this happened."

"It defies logic."

"Tell me about it. My buddy Wyatt works at a communications outfit. He told me he's heard there's going to be a full-blown offensive any day now to try to root the cells out of the city. It's going to be a mess."

"I think half of our apartment building has fled."

"Must be nice."

"Landlord asked if we were leaving. I asked him where he thought we should go. He stared at me with this dumb look on his face like he realized what a stupid question it was. Just about everywhere seems to be like this. Not much escape at this point. Besides, this is home."

"Home," Coop snorts. "We had everything here. And now it's all turned to shit for what?" Because these little babies are afraid of change and the future. What a joke."

We drive to the checkpoint. Coop rolls down his window as a soldier approaches.

"We're here for the solar work," Coop says, holding up his phone for the soldier to scan. I lean over so he can scan my phone too. The soldier waits for a confirmation from the screen on his wristwatch. Once it flashes green, he presses a button, and the blockade opens.

"Park in the lot up there," the soldier says, pointing. "The guys will show you the spot."

Coop coasts until he finds a place to park. We hop out and grab our gear from the back. The storefront windows in this sector are blown out. Bullet holes line the brick walls. A roped-off car is still smoldering from what looks like a bomb blast. Leftist soldiers stand in a loose perimeter at the mouths of each street entrance. A tall guy, almost as tall as me, saunters over. He's got a crew cut and is clean-shaven, wearing khaki pants with a tucked-in navy blue button-down. A Glock and a piss stick dangle from his belt. His jaw works over a piece of gum like he just downed five energy drinks.

"I'm John Eastman. Are you the solar repair guys?"

"That's us," I tell him.

"Great. Come on this way."

"Looks like you guys saw some action last night," Coop says.

"The fuckers are everywhere. More than we were hoping. They're dug in deep. Deeper than a tick on a dog's ass."

"Are we safe here?" I ask.

"Yeah. You should be."

Coop and I exchange glances. 'Should be' aren't the most assuring words to hear regarding your safety in a conflict zone. Eastman leads us to a solar field that takes up an entire city block. Inside is a sea of solar panels angled towards the southern sun. A ten foot high black barred fence surrounds the area. A guard opens a gate and lets us in. We follow Eastman to the patch of panels struck by the rocket. The gate appears intact and seems sturdy enough to withstand a blast. I scan the skyline and spot a section blown out of a building. The trajectory looks right for where the rocket must have traveled. Based on the state of the crumbling building, it doesn't seem like the Left is holding back anymore in dealing with the insurgents.

"Here's the spot," Eastman says. "From our initial assessment, the damage didn't look too severe. We counted three complete units that look to have taken the brunt of the impact and maybe four or five surrounding them that took some damage. Some of the wirings look to have gotten fucked too. The reduced resources are causing a three-block outage. Every hour we're down allows the Righties to coordinate without surveillance. How quickly do you think you guys can finish?"

"We'll get in there now and let you know," I say. "Hang tight for five minutes."

Coop and I walk amongst the panels assessing the severity of the damage. He scopes out the wiring, and I get a sense of how many panels are out. I pull a tablet out of my bag and log into the server. Four are completely out of service, and four need partial repairs. Coop circles around and meets me where the rocket hit.

"What do you think?" I ask.

"Not horrible. It looks like the blast fried at least ten feet of wire. We'll have to rerun a decent length of it, but it's manageable."

We find Eastman. He's chewing away on his gum and says, "Well?"

"I'd say four hours to play it safe," I tell him. "Might be a little sooner than that, but it's always difficult to judge until you start taking things apart."

I can tell he doesn't like my assessment. He spits his gum onto the ground.

"That's a long time for us to sit here," he says.

"It takes what it takes. I just want to give you realistic expectations."

Eastman turns and presses the pod in his ear as he paces. "Hang on," he says. He has a brief conversation and then returns.

"You've got three hours. And if we have to move, there are no asking questions. You get your asses out of there, and we're gone. Understand?"

"You're sure we're safe here, right?" Coop asks.

Eastman takes out a packet of gum, unwraps two pieces, and crams them in his mouth before answering.

"Three hours," he says. He eyes the damage one last time, then heads off.

Coop and I go to the truck to gather the rest of the supplies we need for the job.

"That guy seem a little on edge to you?" Coop says.

"A bit, yeah."

"Bet he knows something we don't."

"Let's do this thing then so we can get out of here."

It takes us three trips to get everything into the lot. I radio into headquarters to kill power to our grid. Coop gets his meter out, hovering it over the lines until it falls silent. He gives me a thumbs up, and we start dismantling the connections.

"So, how's Isla been after the last operation?" Coop says. "What's it been now, four months?"

"Yeah. She's alright, I guess. It's hard to tell sometimes

with her. She keeps things close to the vest. I think she blames herself."

"Shit, really? That's not something you can control. It's not her fault."

"That's what everyone tells her. I think that just pisses her off, though."

"You guys going to keep trying, or you think you're going to throw in the towel?"

"I don't know. I think we're going to give it one more go. If it doesn't happen, then I think that'll be it. She doesn't want to go through the fertilization stuff; honestly, I don't blame her. So we'll see."

"Well, if it comes to that, you two are welcome to take one of ours."

I laugh. "Four's a lot."

"Four's a lot," Coop sighs. "It's tough being so irresistible."

I cut some wires and coil them on the ground.

"So, which kid would you send us?" I ask.

He hesitates, then we say in unison, "Rory."

Coop says, "I swear you'd think that kid eats gunpowder for breakfast and washes it down with crack. I mean, she's out of her goddamn mind."

"She's a wild spirit, no doubt about that."

"Wild? Some days I think Jenny banged Satan. I don't know how else you explain that kid."

"She'll grow out of it."

"I hope so. Otherwise, I'll be in an early grave."

I chuckle and keep working. We make solid progress in the first hour, so we take a water break. As we sit there, I scan the area through the slats in the gate. The bustle of activity has increased since we arrived. Two of the street entrances no longer have soldiers stationed at them, and another group of soldiers huddles around a Humvee. It looks like they are studying a screen. Five soldiers jog over from another street. I spot Eastman thirty yards off. He's pointing and shouting at different groups of soldiers.

"Think something's up?" I say.

"I don't know. Could be," Coop replies. "They do seem tense."

"Let's get back to it then and finish up. Something feels off. I don't want to hang around here longer than we have to."

We chug some water; then I work on swapping out panels while Coop replaces some wiring. My fingers work at a speed faster than I would like. Neither of us talks, listening for any signs of distress from the world around us. We do an hour's worth of work in forty-five minutes. Another forty-five, and I estimate we should be done. As I walk toward the gate entrance to get more panels, a noise stops me in my tracks. Automatic gunfire. I freeze and listen. The staccato is muffled, but it's loud enough that I can tell it's relatively close. Eastman appears at the gate, startling me. He's got on a combat helmet now, along with a flak jacket. In his arms is an assault rifle.

He sees me and shouts, "Shit's hit the fan. Get out of there now. Head for the nearest Safety Zone."

Without waiting for a response, Eastman disappears.

"Coop," I yell. "Time to haul ass."

Coop starts packing up his bag, and I do the same. We hustle to the exit when we've got everything loaded on our backs. I peek out from the gate to survey the area. The soldiers are gone. I take a tentative step out, ensuring there's no immediate threat.

"Boy, they took off in a hurry," Coop says.

"Eastman said we should get to one of the Safety Zones."

"Jesus."

A deafening boom goes off in the distance. Both of us flinch from the noise. The ground shivers like a gust of cold air swept across its back. Over the tops of buildings to the south, a plume of thick black smoke reaches for the sky.

My stomach tightens. Sirens bellow out.

"I think that was near Isla's school," I say, feeling panic surge into my chest.

"Hurry. Get in the truck," Coop shouts. "I'll drive you there."

We run and dive into the truck. Coop fires the engine and starts up the street, then jams on the brakes as a Jeep filled with Righties laying down a steady stream of gunfire blows past the intersection. Coop shifts into reverse and backs up as a Humvee of pursuing Lefties rumbles by. I can feel the shockwaves in my chest as their .50-caliber machine gun pumps out rounds. Coop swings the truck in an arch then cranks the shifter into drive and lurches forward. People are fleeing in all directions as we barrel out from the side street onto a main artery. Broken glass litters the pavement. A handful of motionless bodies splayed out on the ground, blood forming tiny swimming pools beneath them.

At the next intersection, I glance down the street to the right to see a bus engulfed in flames. A charred half-naked woman is screaming, frantically waving her shirt to try and extinguish a fire consuming a man writhing on the ground. I tamp down the urge to puke. The sirens wail. Car horns blare. Gunfire reverberates off the brick walls. Coop keeps his foot on the gas, whipping past a strip of stores that people have begun to loot—mixed amongst the chaos, pockets of people brawling.

Two blocks ahead, we see another burning bus blocking

the road. Coop spins the wheel, making a hard left turn. He swerves to avoid a three-car pile-up, sending the truck onto the sidewalk. People dive out of the way.

"WatchOutWatchOut," I say as Coop misses flattening a woman by a hair.

I clutch the armrest and hang on for dear life as the truck bounces back onto the road. Coop accelerates through the street. We're about half a mile from Isla's school as another intersection appears. Coop lays on the horn, keeping it depressed as he floors the pedal, hurtling us through the intersection. I look over Coop's shoulder and spot a Leftie Humvee. If we were two seconds slower, we would've collided with them. I turn around just in time to see a spiraling cloud attached to the tail of a rocket whistle over our truck. The rocket connects with the Humvee in a thunderous concussion that shatters Coop's window.

"Holy shit," Coop yells. He's hunched forward, almost hugging the steering wheel.

"Are you ok?"

Coop slings the truck to the right, cutting into a narrow side street out of the direct line of the melee. He slows down, patting himself with one hand.

"Yeah, I think I'm alright," he stutters out. "You good?"

"My fucking ears are ringing."

Coop edges forward, checking his rearview mirror.

"Pull over," I say. "I'll get out here and do the rest on foot."

"I'll get you there. There's not much more to go."

"I appreciate it, but it's too dangerous. Can't risk something happening to you because of me. Get home to your family. I'll be alright."

Coop thinks about this. I can tell he doesn't like it.

"Are you sure?"

"Yes," I say as I pop the door to get out. "If phones are still working, text me to let me know you're safe."

"Ezra," he says.

I look at him.

"Good luck," he says.

I nod. "You too."

I slam the door shut. The truck speeds off and disappears around the next corner. In my head, I map out the quickest route to Isla's school, then take off running. At the next crossroad, I peer around the edge of a building to assess the situation. The street is mostly empty. I hear sporadic gunfire to the left, so I go straight. I cut through a parking lot, crouching beside cars to avoid attracting attention to myself. Twenty yards away, an armed Rightie runs past me at the border of the lot. I drop to my stomach and slide under an SUV. Shouts follow, then gunfire. I can see the lone Rightie is trapped. He goes to his knee, and before he can raise his rifle, a hail of bullets tears into him. His body jerks under the impact, then a round finds his skull, and he pitches forward. Three Lefties run up to the dead guy. One of them unholsters a pistol and fires a confirmation round into the already dead guy's face. Then they hustle off. I get to my feet and sprint toward the twice-killed Rightie. I leap over the bits of his skull and brain sprawled across the pavement.

Isla's school is the next block over. I run, stop, and check for signs of troops. Run, stop, check. As I get closer, the screaming and the cries of little kids hit me. Two yellow buses sit stationary in front of the school. Smoke billows out from a high rise across the street. It must be what got hit in the explosion I heard. Firefighters pour water into the blaze. Cars clustered at odd angles surround the building. Three Humvees are alongside the school buses. A few Leftie soldiers hunker down next to the Humvees forming a perimeter. Another batch of Lefties are helping to get kids, parents, and teachers onto the buses. A mother sits on the curb, her shirt saturated with blood from a lifeless child in her arms. Next to her, a Leftie medic works on a child while his parents hold each other, sobbing. The scene is so surreal that I'm unsure if I'm awake. Something this horrific can't happen in the real world, can it? And not here. Not America.

My feet won't move as torment floods my senses. Isla, my brain says. Find Isla. Go. I brush past the human agony and head for the main entrance. I approach a Leftie soldier.

"Where are all the teachers?" I ask.

"Step back, sir," the soldier shouts.

"Sorry," I say, holding up my hands. "My wife works here. I need to find her."

"I have no fucking clue, man. Our focus is on the kids. We're cataloging them here as best we can."

"Are people still inside?"

"I think so. People went in to sweep each of the rooms. I'm sure there are teachers there helping."

I dart away from the soldier. I hear him shouting something at me, but I don't turn back. The school is a decent size, but I'm lucky it's only a single level. I go left, racing to Isla's classroom. I swing open the door and scan it, only seeing sleeping musical instruments. She's not here. I head into the hallway, continuing towards the back of the school, quickly checking in each room as I go. I start calling out her name. My pace quickens as I pass room after room. I head down the next hallway, and at the end of it, I see a group of people. Please let her be there. Please let her be there. I skid to a stop. I recognize one of the women.

"Brit," I say.

She turns to me, her eyes wide, filled with fear and confusion. Her clothes are dusty, and her face is pale. It takes her a second to recognize me.

"Ezra. Oh my god, what are you doing here?"

"Where's Isla? Is she here?"

"Isla," she says, rolling the name over her tongue like a mint.

I take her by the arm. "Brit, look at me. Is my wife alive?"

She comes out of the daze for a moment, blinking. "Yes. Yes, she's here. She was at the nurse's office the last I saw her."

"The nurse's office. Perfect. Thank you."

I shuffle through the small gathering of people and head for the nurse's office. Twenty feet from the office, my foot slips off to the side. I stop myself from falling but notice a dark substance smeared on the floor. As I walk a few steps forward, I realize it's blood. A trail leads down the hall as if someone dragged a wounded animal across the floor. My heart is jackhammering against my chest. Moans seep from the room. I hold my breath and walk in. A nauseating scent of bodily fluids and rubbing alcohol hangs thick in the air. Bodies pack the space. A woman I recognize as the principal is standing over a young boy lying on the exam table. She's holding a towel on his blood-stained forehead. Sitting at the foot of the table is another boy with his back against the wall. He's holding an ice pack to his cheek and looks like he might throw up. Two adults I don't know are on the floor, one attending to the other. At the back of the room, by the window, I see her.

"Isla," I shout.

She turns at my voice, and a smile breaks across her face

when she sees me. I cut through the crowd of people and wrap her in a huge hug. I want to say something, but I can't. My throat clogs with emotion. She pushes back from me, tears in her eyes.

"What are you doing here?" she says.

"I heard the explosion. I...I thought I'd lost you."

She places her hand on my cheek and gently kisses me.

"Are you hurt?" I ask.

"No. Some people were outside when the blast went off, and part of the gym collapsed. The soldiers and fire trucks showed up and started to organize an evacuation. I stayed to help clear the rooms and tend to anyone injured."

I then notice a small girl seated on a short stool behind my wife. The girl is between eight and ten years old. She has a slender frame with brownish-red hair pulled back with clips. One of the clips is missing from the left side of her head, giving her soft features an asymmetrical look. She's wearing a jean dress over rainbow striped leggings with gauze wrapped around her forearm. She looks at me through vibrant green eyes.

"Hello," I say.

"This is Harper," Isla says.

Harper gives me a half smile as a soldier appears in the doorway.

"The rest of the building is clear," he shouts. "Everyone else needs to leave now. If you are injured, there are paramedics outside. If you are a child and your parents haven't come for you, you are to board one of the school buses. They will take you to Safety Zone C. Anyone else is to return home or go to one of the Safety Zones. Let's move."

Two soldiers file into the room and carry out the boys on the exam table. The people on the ground stagger to their feet.

I look at the little girl.

"Is it alright if I carry you?"

She looks at Isla, who gives her a reassuring nod.

"It's alright," Isla says.

Harper whispers, "Ok."

I lift her off the stool like he weighs as much as a down pillow, cradling her in my arms. Isla is next to me as we emerge from the school. The chaos and the misery rage on.

"Don't look," I tell Harper.

She clutches my shirt and buries her face in my chest. We get in line for one of the school buses. When our turn comes, I place the girl on the second step of the bus. She doesn't say anything, but her eyes are afraid.

"It'll be ok," I say.

I step out of the way so the next person can board. I watch as Harper drifts into the cavern of the bus. In a slow trudging crawl, the buses leave. I feel a tremor in the ground that I assume is from the weight of the vehicles moving in unison, but then I hear panicked shouting. The bombed-out highrise gives a last shudder, then collapses in on itself. The sound is like a stampede of horses running straight through my brain. We're about fifty yards from the rising cloud of debris. I grab Isla's hand and break for the first clear direction I see away from the destruction. The fog swallows the echoes of screams. I glance back and see the gray plume closing in on us. We won't be able to outrun it.

Across the street, I see two abandoned cars ensnared.

"Follow me," I shout.

We sprint for the cars. The first one's passenger window is smashed, but the second car is intact. I throw open the back door of the sedan, waving for Isla. She dives into the back seat, and I follow her, slamming the door as the debris cloud consumes us. The car rocks back and forth. I can't see anything but a dark tan color as if we're being buried on a beach. We cling to each other, gasping for air from the exertion. I hope the glass will hold up. We sit there, holding on for what feels like forever. Gradually, the interior of the car starts to brighten. Out the front windshield, faint outlines of buildings appear.

"I think it's starting to clear," I say.

Isla sits up, "Yeah, it looks like it."

I fish out my Leatherman, open the knife, and then slip the blade into the sleeve of my uniform near my bicep. The knife glides through until I've cut the sleeve off, then I do the same for the other side.

"What are you doing?" Isla says.

"We don't want to be breathing that stuff. This should work as a makeshift mask to get us home."

I sever the connecting stitching of the arm sleeves and unfurl the fabric. I cut matching L-shapes out of the left, leaving a square for the face and dangling strips to tie around our heads.

"Hold this in place," I say, handing her one of the crude masks.

She stretches it over her face; then, I pinch the fabric where her eyes are, cut slashes to see through, and give it back to her. We tie them on and despite the situation, can't help but laugh at how ridiculous we look.

"Quite the fashion statement," Isla says. "New York Fashion Week, here we come."

I grin, "Come on, let's get out of here."

An eerie quietness surrounds us. The fog has mostly settled, leaving a layer of soot on the ground. The sun peeks through the space where the highrise once stood. Isla faces the school, lingering on it as if she's saying goodbye to part of herself. Sensing her thoughts, I say, "You'll be back again."

She sighs and says, "I'm ready to go home."

We head east, holding our masks tight to our faces. They're not perfect, but they filter out the bulk of the dust that still floats in the air.

"Do you think the apartment will be safe? Or should we go to one of the Safety Zones?" Isla shouts through her mask.

"We can try the apartment. If it seems like a no-go, I think Safety Zone F isn't much farther from there."

"Ok."

We stick close to the buildings as we navigate home, ducking into side alleys or alcoves at the sound of gunfire. My knife is in my hand, ready to strike if needed. Every minute or so, I look at Isla, making sure she's still with me. An irrational fear goads me into thinking if I look away for too long, she'll disappear. Three more blocks, and we'll be home. When we're far enough away from the fog, we toss our masks. A taste of chalky metal coats the inside of my mouth. I try to spit but can't summon enough saliva. Two blocks left. A burst of gunfire rings out. It's close. We crouch beside a car and wait.

I whisper, "The shots sounded like they came from George Street. Let's cross here and go down Chapel."

Isla nods.

"I'll follow you," I say.

Isla peers over the car's hood and then creeps to the front. She walks out, takes a step, then leaps to the side, letting out an involuntary scream.

"Ohmygod," she murmurs into her hands.

I rush to her side and track her eyes to the pavement. A small old man lies on his back, each of his limbs twisted into angles that they aren't supposed to go. Split bones pop out of his clothes. His blank eyes gaze to the heavens as his mouth hangs open. From the looks of the injuries and where he is in the street, he probably got run over. One of the Humvees maybe.

I step in front of Isla, blocking her view of the carnage.

"Keep moving," I say.

"He...he...he..."

"I know. Come on."

Half carrying her, I lead her away. A faint sound of a large vehicle accelerating pings my ear. I stop and listen. It's coming towards us. Whoever was doing the shooting might have heard Isla scream and is coming to investigate. It's likely the Lefties, but I don't want to take any chances to find out. All it'd take is one soldier with an itchy trigger finger to think we're Righties, and it's lights out.

"Isla, listen to me. I think someone's coming. We need to run now. You're faster than me. If I lag behind, don't stop. Don't wait. Just get to the apartment."

"I won't leave you."

The vehicle is getting closer. I take Isla's hand and start running. She is hesitant at first, but then she hears the vehicle approaching and commits to the mad dash for home. I'm with her for the first block, but then her track and field days from high school kick in, and she turns on the afterburners. I lose sight of her for a second as she rounds the corner of our block. My heart is in overdrive, and I dig in, pumping my legs and arms. Don't lose her. Run, damn it. I skid around the corner. She's at the door to the apartment building. She has it propped open and is waving me on. As soon as I reach her, she darts in, and I run after her up the stairs. We get to our door, and she's smooth with the key. We spill into the apartment. I fling the door shut and slam the deadbolt home.

The apartment is quiet except for the sounds of our labored breathing. A modicum of safety relaxes my muscles. I pace the living room, trying to steady my breath. Isla grabs two bottles of water and tosses me one. I guzzle it. Nothing has tasted better in my life. I then notice the coating of dust on our clothes.

"We should get out of these," I say. "I'll check if the water is still working."

I slide back the shower curtain and turn the shower dial. A steady stream of water pours out of the head.

"We're in business," I shout out to Isla.

As the water warms up, I peel my feet out of my boots, then strip naked. I hop in the shower. The water hits my skin, washing away the grime. If only it could wash away everything I saw today.

The shower curtain crinkles, and I feel Isla's hands slip under my arms, holding my chest, her body tight against mine. I rotate in her arms so I'm facing her. Before I can say anything, her lips find mine. They're warm and full. Her hands intertwine around the base of my neck. My hands slip under her thighs and I lift her. She locks her lips on mine as our bodies connect. I never want to leave this moment. I never want to leave her. I never want her to be away from me again. We've done this before, many times, but something about this feels different. I realize that for the first time in a long time, I'm painfully aware of how thankful I am to be alive. I guess it's easy to take the little things in life for granted when death isn't knocking at your door.

WEEK 1 - SEPTEMBER 21

An alert on our phones goes off, waking us from a restless sleep.

The time says it's ten in the morning. Isla stirs and snatches her phone, silencing it. The screen buzzes and flashes the transmission of an emergency message. I roll over and nudge Isla.

"I think we're getting an update," I say.

She groans and readjusts herself so that her head is lying on my chest, and she can see the phone. I tap the screen, accepting the transmission. An image of Governor Brubane—the last Governor to be elected when voting still mattered—appears. Her skin is paler than usual, made even fairer by the royal blue blazer she's wearing. Her signature hairstyle of shaved sides with a short top slicked back is disheveled. The bags under her eyes expose that she hasn't slept in a while. Translucent gray eyes stare into the camera. From the looks of it, she's in the Capitol building, but it's hard to tell. Exhaustion riddles her deep voice.

"Citizens of this great city, as many of you already know, an armed conflict with the Right commenced yesterday. The death toll is unknown. We are in a state of emergency. If you are missing someone, please refer to the Missing Persons Bureau link attached to this post for more information. The current directive is to go to one of the designated Safety Zones or shelter in place. Our initial assessment remains stalwart that the groups responsible are vastly outnumbered and will be captured or eliminated in a matter of weeks, allowing you to resume normal activities. Until then, the borders to the city will be closed. No one will be allowed to leave the city limits unless authorized. Please again refer to the links attached for more information and exemptions.

"Over the coming weeks, the military presence will be high. To avoid civilian casualties as much as possible, every citizen remaining inside the city must complete the Democratic

Allegiance Authorization Protocol, or DAAP, within the next twenty-four hours. For the sake of transparency, we'll run the protocol through TURING to remove human bias or prejudice. If you pass, your activation will automatically update on your phone. Failure to comply will hinder our ability to guarantee the safety of each citizen. The authorization will grant you access to limited internet usage, status updates, admittance to the food depots, and your clearance to move more freely throughout the city without incident. Upon successful authorization, your phone must always be on you if leaving your home or a Safety Zone. This step will make it easier for our soldiers to identify who you are and keep any unwanted accidents to a minimum.

"Thank you for your patience and understanding. This threat to freedom and democracy will soon be at an end. Until then, be safe."

The video ends on a seal of the Governor's office.

"Jesus," Isla says. "What do you think?"

"It makes me a little nervous that whether or not we're considered a homegrown terrorist is being decided by a machine."

"It's been proven to be more reliable than humans. We've been fine in the past. It shouldn't be a problem for us anyway."

"That's true. It's just tough sometimes being old enough to remember when our digital lives had a shred of privacy."

"For what, like a day. Everyone knew that wasn't going to last. 'If you've done nothing wrong…'"

"'Then you've got nothing to hide.'" I frown. "Yeah, yeah. I remember the stupid school pledge."

"Should we do it now, to just get it over with?"

I sigh. "Might as well. You go first. I'll make coffee."

Her warm body rolls away from me as she grabs her phone.

I get out of bed and pull on a pair of jeans and a t-shirt. Thoughts of yesterday keep trying to worm their way into the forefront of my mind. It takes more effort than I'd like to push aside the images of bodies, blood, pain, and misery. Keeping my hands busy is how I plan to block the visuals. I grind the beans, set up the mugs, and fire up the water. While I wait, I stroll over to the window and peek out from behind the curtains. The normally bustling streets are empty, as if a giant broom swept everything away. A lonely sensation hollows out my chest looking at the absent signs of life. It's as if we're the last people on earth.

I finish the coffee and return to the bedroom. Isla is out of bed wearing a loose t-shirt, short enough that I can see her underwear. She's staring out the window, too, and doesn't look at me as I put the coffee on the nightstand.

"It's weird how quiet it seems out there," Isla says.

"I was thinking the same thing."

From her gaze, I can tell her thoughts are drifting to what happened yesterday.

"How did the protocol go?" I ask.

She's quiet for a moment, then turns from the window, and says, "I passed. You're stuck with me for a while longer."

I smile at the joke as I sit on the edge of the bed and grab my phone. A few taps here and there, and the protocol boots up. The TURING logo appears along with the message 'protocol syncing. Accessing EZRA ASHER database.'

The loading symbol loops, as the most sophisticated artificial intelligence ever known to man cycles through every piece of my digital life since birth. Analyzing each app, every website, every book, every movie, and every click I've ever made. It's purported that the TURING has crunched so much data about human behavior it could fill a galaxy. By going through my digital record and answering a few questions, it will know me better than I know myself. Human arrogance makes me distrust it, distrust that our creations can outsmart us. The protocol finishes loading. A disclaimer pops up next, telling me to answer the questions honestly. I don't know if I believe it, but I've heard that TURING can detect lies with ninety-nine percent accuracy. The questions are short and to the point; I answer them from the heart. I shouldn't be afraid, but part of me doubts myself being judged by something that can supposedly see to the core of my thoughts. The machine doesn't care about the complexities of what makes me who I am. It has a task, and it does it without bias. It has no feeling about what the output of the one word it deems me, Left or Right, and the effect it will have on my life. Do I want freedom to the extent of others? Do I believe in democracy? Am I a bigot, a racist, or a misogynist? I hold my breath and wait for it to tell me.

Another loading screen appears, then flashes green. The words Authorization Approved stand in big, bold letters next to a checkmark. My shoulders sag in relief. A notification blips. I tap it, and the city app opens, congratulating me on my successful approval. I scroll around the app for a few seconds, then stop on an icon of a map. Tapping it opens a satellite view of the city. It's divided into a ten-by-ten grid with the numbers one through ten running along the top and side. Each grid square has a color. A key at the bottom explains that the blue squares represent locations in the city secured by the Left. Dark gray squares mean the area is off-limits to civilians. Green means it's a Safety Zone, and red means the threat of the Right controlling it is highly probable. The entire border of the map is blue. Each Safety Zone takes up two grid squares, and there are four of them. In the center, four blue blocks indicate the Capitol, and two squares on each side are dark gray for restricted areas. A small circle in the top right corner of the screen has '60%' in the middle showing the current control that the Left has on the city.

I find our apartment building on the map, in grid square 7-6 or sector 14. No color is on our square, meaning the government doesn't know who the hell lives there yet. Patches of red surround us, which doesn't bode well. Forty percent of the city is considered the wild west. It sounds like a relatively small number. Seeing what I saw yesterday makes me believe the government doesn't understand what they're fighting. Ending things in a few weeks feels optimistic. I stuff my phone in the nightstand drawer, thinking if it's not visible, then the problems it can show me won't be either. Isla gazes out the window again, humming a tune. It's something she does when she's far off somewhere.

"You want to play a game?" I ask.

"What?" she says, breaking her attention from the outside world. "A game? What game?"

"I don't know. Any game. Scrabble, poker, chess. I think we've got some others around here."

"Shouldn't we be, I don't know, prepping?"

"Prepping. I think we're past that point. Don't you? That's usually something you do before shit hits the fan, not while the shit's already in the fan and flying around the room."

"That's a pleasant visual."

"We've got supplies for at least the week, don't we? We've got authorization, so hopefully, getting stuff when needed shouldn't be an issue. Probably safer to stay inside until things calm down out there."

"I guess so," she trails off.

I don't want to bring it up, but I do anyway.

"Do you want to talk about yesterday?" I say.

She mulls the question over, then shakes her head, "No. I kind of want to forget yesterday ever happened."

"Ok," I say. "I'm here if you ever want to."

She looks at me, smiles, and whispers, "I know." As she walks toward me, she says, "Find the cribbage board. That was a game I always enjoyed whooping your ass in."

I chuckle. "Oh, ok. It's like that? I see. Challenge accepted."

The cribbage board hides under a pile of crap in the closet. I yank it out and dust it off. Isla clears a spot on the coffee table. She disappears back into the bedroom. I hear sounds of rooting and shuffling under the bed. In her hands is a mini speaker and an ancient iPod.

"I haven't seen that relic in years," I say.

"Since we're playing a game from a long time ago, we might as well kick it old school with our music."

"I like your style. I think alcohol wouldn't hurt either."

"Yes. Lots of alcohol."

Out of a cabinet, I grab two tumbler glasses and a bottle of red wine, a pinot noir. I was never much of a wine drinker, but the red ones were always manageable. After depositing the booze on the table, I make a platter of cheese and crackers with some fresh strawberries and apple slices. We settle in by the table, sitting cross-legged. Isla fires up the speaker and iPod. Horn instruments fill the room with sounds from Nino Rota's score to the Godfather.

"That'll do nicely," she says.

The cork slips out of the wine bottle with a satisfying pop. I fill our glasses halfway. We clink and take a sip. I crack open the deck of cards, shuffling to the melancholic melody. The whole scene reminds me of college when things were simpler. When we were poor, and we made our own fun as cheaply as we could—lost in the comfort of dim lights and easy conversation. Scars from broken homes filled our pasts, but together we made each other whole. The thought of almost losing her yesterday makes today feel like Isla's come into my life anew. She's my world, and I like to think I'm hers.

I deal the cards. Isla finishes her wine and pours more as she taps her fingers to the music. If we didn't have to pretend the world wasn't crumbling around us, this would almost be nice.

Chapter 3

There's a knock on the door, and I open it. Standing in the hallway are two parents still left in the building, each with a child in front of them. Isla came up with the idea to exchange music lessons for rations if people couldn't pay cash. She devoted two days last week to handcrafting flyers to slip under every door in the building, thirty-two in total. She had no idea how many apartments still had people living in them, but she didn't want anyone to miss out. Her thoughtfulness is one of the things I love about her the most.

I don't recognize the people in front of me other than seeing them in passing. The guy on the left introduces himself as Isaac. He's middle-aged like me, a bit shorter with a classic dad bod. A baggy t-shirt with several holes in it stretches over the paunch of his gut. He wears glasses, but they don't fit his face very well, and the way he continually touches them, it seems like he's not accustomed to wearing them. Contact wearer maybe and can't easily get them anymore, so he's resorted to glasses. With him is a boy, James, who's about nine or ten. James looks excited to be anywhere new, even though he's now going into an identical apartment.

The other parent is a woman who tells me her name is Emilia. Her black hair is frazzled, and she looks at me with exhaustion. She talks quickly and seems eager to unload her kid so she can find someplace to hide and cry. Desperation seeps out of her pores. I feel bad for thinking that and avoid her eyes. Her child is a girl, Mia, who is about the same age as James. She wears her hair in a tight braid and shrinks back slightly, seeing me in the doorframe. Isla comes up behind me and introduces herself with a warm smile. The children smile back, and she welcomes them into the apartment.

"Be back in an hour or so," Isla tells the parents.

"You're a godsend," Emilia says. Without waiting to say goodbye to her daughter, she jams a plastic bag into my hand and takes off like she thinks Isla is about to change her mind. In the bag are two water bottles and a roll of toilet paper; her payment for the lesson. Isaac and I watch her disappear down a hallway. He hands me a plastic bag with his barter payment of batteries and a few boxes of pasta. The boy waves to his dad, and the three enter the living room.

"I appreciate you guys doing this," Isaac says. "We've both been going stir-crazy. He couldn't wait for today. I always hated school growing up, but he really misses it."

"I can imagine."

Isaac lingers in the hallway, then says, "Hey, I was gonna go up to the roof and have a smoke. You're more than welcome to join me. It'd be great to talk to an adult for a change."

I'm considering saying no, but then I hear the ping of Isla's electric keyboard come to life and say, "Sure, why not." I shout to Isla. "I'll be back in a little bit."

She shouts back, "Ok."

On the roof, Isaac ducks down.

"What are you doing?" I ask, starting to regret my decision to come with him.

"Snipers," he says. "Never know where they are."

I scan the surrounding buildings for any possible perches for a sniper. There are definitely plenty of spots for one to be hiding. I can't tell if Isaac's messing with me, but then I think it'd be a pretty stupid way to die, so I crouch and follow him to a section of the roof where large air conditioning units shield us from any direct line of fire. We sit on the ground with our backs against the metal of the units. Isaac roots around in his pocket and pulls out a metal tin that contains loose-leaf tobacco and white rolling papers.

"I'd quit smoking years ago," he says. "When all this shit broke out, my wife left me. She said I was too liberal." He laughs, shaking his head as he sprinkles the tobacco into the paper and rolls a sad-looking cigarette. "I lost my job soon after that, and she left me with James. I figured, fuck it. What do I have to lose? I could be shot or blown up tomorrow. Might as well do something I enjoy until then."

He pulls out a vibrant red lighter and flicks the flame to life. When the cigarette burns, he offers me the tin.

"Want one?"

"I'm good."

"You don't want to know what I had to trade to get this," he laughs again. "Any nicotine product is worth its weight in gold out there right now."

"I bet."

Isaac stares into the sky as he smokes. Halfway through the cigarette, he says, "You hear about that shit happening in Georgia?"

"No. I haven't been reading much. Access has been a bit spotty. Even when I can, I get too angry, then I get depressed. What happened down there?"

"Fighting started in Atlanta, two days after it started here. Guess the Righties blew up some building, and the reports said it was worse than the Oklahoma City bombing from way back. So then a retaliation bomb went off that leveled an entire city block. The Left blamed it on a faction army, but it sounded like it was a hard-core bomb the government dropped. Who knows, though, it's hard to tell what's real anymore."

He inhales another drag, then exhales.

"I knew America wouldn't last forever, but damn I didn't think we were just going to blow everything to hell in the process." He falls quiet then, lost in thought, then he glances at me and says, "You got any kids?"

"We tried for a while, but it's not seeming like it's in the cards for us."

"Eh, you're probably better off," he says as he taps some ash off the end of the dwindling cigarette. "I love the kid, don't get me wrong, but I feel bad for him. Kids shouldn't have to grow up like this. And what am I supposed to do? He looks to me for answers. He wants me to be strong and not afraid. But I don't have answers, and I'm just as scared shitless as he is. It's a garbage feeling to see disappointment in your kid's eyes. And when he says he's hungry, I can't give him a straight answer as to when we'll get a good meal again. So, consider yourself lucky."

Part of me wants to punch this guy in the side of the head. Self-righteous asshole. He doesn't know what we've been through to generalize like that, to put his insecurities on our situation. I'm about to leave, and I think Isaac senses my thoughts because he grinds out his cigarette and half laughs, half sobs. "Sorry, don't listen to me. That's mostly the divorce talking."

"It's alright," I sigh, now just feeling bad for the guy. He looks like he could crack any second. "Everyone's just trying to make it through."

He flicks the stub of the cigarette away. "I thought the pandemic was bad, but this...where do we go from here?"

I don't have an answer, so I don't say anything. My silence seems to make him uncomfortable. Isaac nods then moves to a crouched position. "I should get back down there. I've got some things to do before your wife's lesson ends."

"Alright," I say, staying seated. "I think I'm going to enjoy the air while I can."

He studies me for a moment and sort of frowns. "Well, I'll see you around, I guess. Thanks for listening."

I nod, which sets him on his way to shuffling to the roof door. He closes it behind him like he's trying not to wake a sleeping baby. I think about his question, 'Where do we go from here?' as the sun creeps out from behind a cloud. If Isaac is any indicator of what frame of mind people will be in when this ordeal is over, where we're going won't be pretty.

WEEK 6 - OCTOBER 26

Gunfire jolts me from a dead sleep. I roll off the bed, sticking low to the floor. The shots sound like they're only two blocks away. Isla squirms across the mattress and then drops next to me. I wrap her tight in my arms. We're five weeks in, and the fighting is intensifying. At week three, the progress map showed the Left had control of eighty-three percent of the city. It seemed like victory was in sight. Maybe a week or two more, but the Left got greedy and took a gamble.

They released a missile into a supposed stronghold of the Right. In countless interviews, the Governor stated over and over again that level of force wouldn't come into the equation. They were confident their ground troops could handle the job. The Left took a calculated risk to wipe out a large faction of the Right. If it had worked and ended the fighting, they figured people would have overlooked the lie that missiles wouldn't be used. But the plan backfired. While the missile killed several high-level Right insurgents, it also collapsed the building next to it, killing sixty civilians, fifteen of which were children. Things spiraled from there. People on the fence of which side to align with went to the Right. Eighty-three percent control plummeted to seventy percent in a week. The number of casualties amongst the entire population spiked.

Isla and I stretched our initial food supply for a week and a half. I ventured out during the second week and could easily restock the essentials. After the missile debacle, it got hairy leaving the apartment. Soldiers were everywhere. Skirmishes would break out in an instant with no warning. One time I was out, a stray bullet almost got me. From that day on, I would only leave the apartment if it was necessary.

Isla taps my forearm urgently.

"Let me go. I think I'm going to puke."

She scrambles over me and rushes into the bathroom, slamming the door behind her. The windows tremble as an RPG explodes nearby. Sounds of multiple .50-cals answer the explosion. Then there's a halt to the gunfire, some shouting, and the city is quiet again. I crawl to the bathroom door and sit to the side of it.

"Are you ok?" I ask.

"Give me a minute."

I daydream while I wait for her. Thinking of the bullets flying a few blocks away, I wonder what it would feel like to get shot. Would it burn? I think I've heard people say it burns when a bullet goes into you. It makes sense, I guess—a tiny piece of metal boring through your skin at over a couple of hundred feet per second. Movies have given me a distorted perception of getting shot. Then I wonder what it must be like to be hit with an RPG. To literally be blown to pieces. It has to be a surreal experience to have something so compact carrying so much force, that it can separate bone and muscle into tiny pieces. I wonder how long the pain must last. I've heard of instantaneous death, but what does that really mean? One second you're you; the next, you're not. It's crazy to think how durable humans are to have survived as long as we have as a species, and yet, we can be obliterated in a nanosecond. And the irony is that we're the ones that created the tools to destroy ourselves. I'd laugh if it weren't so goddamn sad.

The door creaks open. Isla spots me on the floor and sits down. She puts her feet on top of mine as she gazes into my eyes. She's been crying.

"You alright?" I ask.

"I'm pregnant," she whispers.

The words roll in my head as I nod, unsure if she's happy or upset.

"You are?" I say, keeping my tone flat, ready to pivot toward one emotion or the other.

"How's that make you feel?"

I shrug, "How does that make you feel?"

She sighs and shrugs, "I just don't want to get my hopes up again."

"I know."

"Then I look outside, and I feel...I don't know...selfish, I guess. Why would we bring an innocent child into this misery? What life can they expect to have?"

"I understand that. This isn't an ideal time, but when is?"

Isla rubs my ankle with her thumb, focusing her attention on the spot.

"What do you want to do?" she asks.

"You know how I feel about it. You know I'd love to have a kid, but I'll support whatever path you want to go down."

"Do you even think we'd be able to see a doctor? You know, to see if this one...if this one is going to stick around."

"Last I checked, the hospitals are still secure. There haven't been any attacks on them. Definitely will be busier, but I'm sure we could see someone."

"It'll be dangerous getting there."

"Yes. It probably will," I concede. "I saw on some message boards that certain doctors come in with military escorts right to your home. I think you've got to pay for it, but we could try that?"

"Can we afford it?"

I doubt it. The prices of food and commodities have skyrocketed. Our small savings account has been depleted, with both of us not working. We could go another two months before we've burnt through that.

"We can make it work," I say. "I'll look into it now."

"Really?"

"For you, of course."

She unfurls her legs, leans into me, and kisses me on the cheek. I can smell the mint from the toothpaste.

"I don't deserve you," she says.

"I hope you remember that when it's time to pick a name for this kid."

Isla grins, "My memory has been known to be selective at times."

"Don't I know it."

She kisses me again, then returns to the bed, pulling the covers over her head. I go into the bathroom and wash up. I lather up with soap, as shaving cream isn't worth the expense. As the weeks drag on, I've noticed more and more how many things in my life were luxuries. How lucky I was. I'm halfway through the shave with a razor three shaves past its prime when the power cuts out. The blackouts are increasing along with the death rate. I string up my solar power camping lantern and finish my shave primarily by feel.

I get dressed and go into the living room to let Isla rest. My phone signal is weak, but I can get on the message boards and track down the doctor escort service. I filter the options to the doctors with the soonest availability, then narrow it down by cost. The most affordable one I can find is Dr. Jada Powell. Her credentials say she worked with the Peace Corps and the Red Cross and 'is no stranger to working in conflict zones.' Three days is the tentative soonest date she could be here. I enter the type of medical service we're looking for, and the site calculates her fee. It's higher than I hoped it would be. If Isla didn't have the history she did with pregnancies, I'd take our chances without seeing someone until the delivery, but I don't want to risk things now. I put in my card information and book the appointment. A notification comes through on my phone.

It thanks me for my payment, then lays out a disclaimer about the arrival date. 'Conflict zones present numerous challenges. While we send our medical staff with highly trained security forces, the fluidity of the crisis is outside of our control. Thank you for your patience and understanding.'

I lock my phone and do the only thing I can, wait.

WEEK 6 - OCTOBER 29

Isla has morning sickness every day after. She's pale, and her lips have an odd purplish hue. A blanket of frailness seems to encapsulate her. When she's not throwing up, she's sleeping. A little soup and some crackers are about all she can stomach. I'm getting worried and check my phone more than I should for updates on when the doctor will arrive. I try to keep busy while Isla sleeps. I do push-ups, sharpen my knife, and clean the apartment even though it doesn't need it. Whenever I stop moving, I start thinking; I start worrying. So I do more push-ups until my arms are jelly.

The days crawl by, and then it's the day the doctor is supposed to arrive. I haven't gotten any updates, which makes me uneasy. I reorganize the cabinets for the fortieth time and drink some coffee. The power comes back on after three days. I don't know how long this will last, so I rush to plug in all of my battery packs and charge my phone. I check the map on the government app. The Left's control of the city is up to seventy-five percent. I question how accurate that number is. The more worrying piece of the map is the other red squares that seem to cluster around our grid number. I hope the doctor will be able to get here.

I scour some news outlet websites. An article pops up about the impact of the elections next week. The integrity of the democratic system lives in a dismal state with the common practice of the losing side disputing the results. I never thought truth and reality would become subjective ideas. The article's author suggests a decisive military blow is imminent if the Left wants to maintain any level of authority and backing before the elections. It's a bleak outlook, but what isn't these days?

The afternoon drags into the night when I finally receive a notification. A brief message says, 'Dr. Powell is five minutes away. Be at your building entrance to meet her.' I dash into the bedroom and rub Isla awake.

"The doctor is going to be here soon. I'm going down to let her in."

She smiles at me and says, "Ok. I'll be ready."

I kiss her on the forehead and run out of the room. I grab my phone and slide the Leatherman into my pocket, just in case, and hustle out of the apartment. My feet barely touch the stairs as I bound down. At the main entrance, I sink into the shadow at the side of the door. I peer out with tempered excitement like a kid waiting for his parents to arrive home from a shelter with a new puppy. Time ticks off in my head. I know I got down here in under five minutes. I scan the area but don't spot anyone. I check the time stamp on the notification and see it's eight minutes past. What if she doesn't come? What if she gets shot on her way here? What would I do then?

A flicker glints in the dark, and I can make out the movement of faint shapes coming toward me. It has got to be them. My hands grip the bar to open the door and almost slip off from the sweat seeping out. Three people ascend the stairs, and I open the door. The person in front is a middle-aged black guy wearing a dark gray baseball cap and a matching dark gray flak jacket with a large white medical cross printed on the front along with the words MEDIC. An assault rifle dangles at his side as he withdraws a handgun and levels it at my face.

"Whoa," I say, holding up my hands defensively. "Easy."

"I need to scan your authorization," the guy says with a controlled calmness.

I keep one hand raised and slowly reach into my pocket and bring out my phone. The guy keeps the gun trained on me while he drops a hand to take hold of his phone. He taps a few times, places it next to mine, and studies the results; then, he lowers the gun.

"He's clear," the guy says.

A woman appears from behind the front guy. She is average height, black, with short braided hair tucked underneath a tactical helmet. A similar flak jacket with white medical cross drapes over her slender frame. Her warm eyes stare into mine as she says, "Mr. Asher?"

"Yes. That's me."

"Let's step inside if you don't mind," she says. "I don't like being out here longer than I have to."

"Right," I say, moving out of the way so the three of them can enter.

"I'm Dr. Powell," she says and extends a hand for me to shake. "That's Duke," pointing at the guy that greeted me. "And that's Ricardo," she says, pointing her thumb over her shoulder at the second guy behind her.

I shake everyone's hand. A scent of cordite and sweat fills the tiny alcove. I lead the group up the stairs.

"Thank you for coming out here. I appreciate it. All of you. How is it out there?" I ask.

"Not good," Duke answers. "We're lucky we got through. This sector is in rough shape. We met a small pocket of resistance two blocks over."

"Oh," I say, not expecting his bluntness. I'm not sure how to respond. A tinge of guilt overcomes me for having these strangers risk their lives for us.

"That'll be enough of that," Powell says.

"Apologies," Duke responds.

"No worries," I say.

I shake it off and bring them into the apartment. Ricardo stays by the door as Duke follows Powell into the living room. Isla is dressed and seated on the couch. She looks like she put on makeup. Powell walks forward, dropping her backpack on the floor next to the couch. Duke moves to a discreet corner.

"I'm Dr. Jada Powell," she says to Isla, sitting next to her on the couch. "A pleasure to meet you."

"Likewise," Isla says. "My name's Isla."

"So I hear we have a baby on the way?" Powell says.

"That's the hope."

Powell pulls a tablet out of her backpack, then a pair of glasses from a pouch on her flak jacket. She skims over the screen.

"You were seeing Dr. Khatri, correct?"

"Yes, that's right."

"And it says here that you've had three miscarriages?"

"Yes."

"How long since your last period?"

"About seven weeks."

"Any bleeding?"

"No."

"Anything else I should know? Any concerns before I start?"

"I've been throwing up a lot. I'm tired and dizzy. I've been feeling weak."

"Noticed any weight loss?"

"Yes."

"Ok. Anything else."

"Not that I can think of."

"Alright, then," Powell says as she places the tablet on the coffee table. "I'm going to draw some blood and test what I can with the devices I have with me. They're quite accurate and quite fast. Once I get that going, I'll run some sonar on you and see what we're working with. Sound like a plan?"

Isla nods, unable to speak. Tears are welling in her eyes. Powell takes her hand.

"It'll be alright," she says. "I know I look like I'm only in my thirties, but I've been doing this for a while. You're in good hands."

Isla smiles, wiping tears away, "It's just been a long road, and I'm afraid of what you're going to tell me tonight."

"I understand. My mom always said, 'suffering was created as a means to appreciate happiness.' Let's just take it one step at a time."

"I know. You're right."

"Of course, I'm always right. Isn't that right, Duke?"

"That's right," Duke says.

Powell rummages through her bag until she finds a blood draw kit.

"Why don't you lie down for me," she says, getting up so Isla can stretch out.

When Isla is comfortable, Powell wraps the tourniquet around Isla's arm, preps the area, and draws four vials with expert precision. She then removes a small white machine that looks like an oversized cue ball with a flat base. With one of her hands under the device and one hand on top, Powell rotates, separating it in half. She loads the four vials, secures the halves together, and then taps a button. The machine whirs to life, eventually settling into a purr as it analyzes the blood. Powell takes out another device along with a set of earbuds.

"Lift your shirt to your chest for me, please," Powell says.

The device chirps and Powell plugs her ears with the buds. She opens a small tube of jelly and lathers it onto Isla's stomach.

"Ready?" Powell says.

Isla's lips are a straight line, but she manages a nod. The device makes contact with her stomach, and Powell slowly maneuvers it over the area, back and forth like a lawnmower. I study Powell's face for any telltale signs of defeat, but she doesn't give anything away. She scans a little longer, then stops. The device stays on the spot, and Powell removes an earbud, holding it out to Isla.

"Go ahead," Powell says.

Isla hesitates, then takes the earbud as if it might bite her. She puts it into her ear. A smile spreads on Isla's face as she looks at me.

"That's your baby's heartbeat," Powell says. "It sounds perfect."

Powell removes the other earbud as she stands up and motions for me to take it. My knees feel like they're locked in place. I stagger over, take the earbud and sit down. Powell places the device back on Isla's stomach, and a steady whump, whump, whump fills my eardrum. It's the most beautiful sound I've ever heard. Powell guides my hand to take the device to keep it in place. She goes to the blood analyzer, presses a button, and then scoops up the tablet again.

"The heartbeat sounds strong and tracks with where you're at in the pregnancy. The blood work shows some imbalances with some of your levels. How has your diet been?"

"The last two weeks haven't been good."

"It's been more challenging to get to the food depots, and when I do, the options are limited," I tell her.

"They usually are," Powell says.

"I have a sample pack I can give you for the nausea that should get you through the night. I'll give you a prescription for more if it continues and you can manage to find a place that will fill it. I'll note in your chart as well some vitamins to take, again, if you can find them. The biggest thing is dehydration. If you let that go too far, it can start causing other issues. Depending on the situation around here, I'd plan on a follow-up in two months."

Isla removes the earbud, and I do the same. I hand them and the device to Powell.

"That's it?" Isla asks.

"That's it," Powell says. "You're going to have a baby. It seems like the fourth time was the magic number. Don't overexert yourself; otherwise, the rest is up to you."

"I don't know what to say," Isla whispers.

"Well, I never get tired of hearing thank you," Powell grins as she packs her gear into her backpack. She places the pill sample pack on the coffee table.

Isla smiles, "Thank you."

"It's my pleasure. Now, if you have any questions, you can send me a message through the app you found me on. I'm usually good at getting back to people in a day or two."

Powell slings her bag on, and Duke comes to her side. I get up and start towards the door. Powell stops me.

"No need," she says. "We can see ourselves out. Good luck to both of you."

On the verge of tears, I shake her hand and croak out a

thank you. She nods with a smile, then heads for the door. They file out of the apartment, and we're alone once again.

I drift back to the couch as if filled with helium. Isla grabs my hand and pulls me in before I float away.

"Are we going to have a kid?" I ask.

"I didn't hear anything she said after I heard that heartbeat."

"That was, is, the loveliest little heartbeat, isn't it."

"It is," Isla says. "I didn't think it was going to happen."

"What do we do now? Should we celebrate?"

"I'll celebrate when I stop puking all over the place."

"Let me get you some water."

I go to the kitchen and put the kettle on. I fill Isla's water bottle, then fix a mug with honey and a tea bag. When the water finishes boiling, I pour it over the bag and stir it. Isla washes the pills down.

"Can I get you anything else?" I ask.

"No, just sit with me."

I drop onto the couch and put my feet on the coffee table. Isla puts a pillow on my lap and lays down. Within minutes she's fast asleep. I sit there in the quiet that's occasionally interrupted by distant gunshots. Amid all of this destruction and death, we created a new life. The thought sticks in my heart as I realize I'm going to be a father.

WEEK 7 - NOVEMBER 3

I find Isla curled up on the floor of the bathroom. She's been like this the last four mornings. I bend down and collect her in my arms. She weighs almost nothing. Her eyes flutter open as I lay her in the bed.

"This is crazy. You can't keep doing this. Please let me try to get the medicine for you."

"I'll be ok," she says.

"You're only getting worse. If we wait any longer, I'm scared of what might happen to the two of you."

"It's too dangerous. If I lose you…I can't raise a baby on my own."

"Well, that logic works both ways, you know."

Her eyes close. She takes deep breaths, each one looking more painful than the next. It kills me to see her like this. I grab my phone and pull up the map.

"Look, the city is eighty percent secured. The odds are in my favor. I'll be careful. I promise."

She peeks at the screen.

"We're surrounded by red."

"It's early. The insurgents are generally not active at this time. I can get through."

"And what if you can't?"

"Then, at least I'll have tried. I'd rather that than do nothing as you waste away." I take her hand as I caress the side of her face. "Please."

She lies there motionless. I can tell she's weighing the risks against how much pain she's enduring.

"No," she says. "I don't want you to go. I can ride this out."

I sigh, "This isn't a good idea. I don't understand why you're being so stubborn. After all we've been through."

"After all I've been through, you mean," she snaps.

"That's not fair."

"You haven't had the procedures. You're not the one puking your guts out. It's not your responsibility to grow something inside of you."

"I get that," I say, trying to control my temper. Isla's hurting, and she's lashing out, and I'm not making it easier on her. I pace the room, annoyed at her comments and frustrated there's so little I can do to help her. Seeing her hurting like this is tearing me up inside. She holds out her hand, beckoning me to her.

"I'm sorry," she says. "It's just... I'm struggling. I'm tired and sick of being sick, you know? But I need you. I need you here with me. Don't you trust me?"

I sigh and shake my head.

She pats the bed. "Come sit with me."

I relent, like always, and sit next to her, still thinking of how I can convince her I'll be alright. She rests her head on my thigh and places a hand on my leg.

"Give me just a few more days," she says.

Resigned, I say, "Fine."

Isla continues to caress my leg until she's drifted off to sleep. After five minutes of sitting there, her breathing shifts into a low steady rhythm, letting me know she's out cold. A thought comes to me, then. I can slip out of the apartment without her knowing I'm gone. I've still got time to get to the pharmacy. She'll be mad when she finds out what I've done, but it'll be worth the heat I'll take from her in the long run. As softly as I can, I slide my leg out from under her, then hold my breath and ease off the bed. I stand there for a few seconds, watching her, ensuring she's still asleep before I leave the room.

I find the prescription from Powell in the kitchen and tuck it into my wallet, where I know it'll be safe. I lace up my sneakers in case I have to run. My trusty Leatherman I take along with my keys. I chug a glass of water and then slip out of the apartment. My route is fresh in my mind. A narrow strip runs west through the Right-controlled territory. I can pick my way through the numerous alleys that should give me good coverage from the main streets. Once I get through the red area, it's seven blocks to the pharmacy. I got a call through to them yesterday, and they confirmed they had the medicine. The only downside is they're open for a small window of time. I've got about an hour to get there. It should be enough.

Outside, the cool morning air takes my breath away. I haven't been out in eight days. My lungs drink it in like they've been living inside a coffin. Overcast clouds hide the sun. At least, I think they're clouds. For all I know, it's smoke from a dying explosion. The streets are empty as I turn left, heading north. At the next intersection, I turn left again. People are milling about. Everyone I see has their eyes focused on their feet as they shuffle along. Everything about the city feels different. The people seem tired. Hell, the buildings even seem tired. Soot clings to every surface, smothering the possibilities for anything to grow. Some people are sleeping on benches—others in ramshackle tents. I spot one guy sitting in the middle of the sidewalk staring at his feet, trying to figure out why they stopped moving. A few storefronts are charred black from bomb blasts. I stare into the hollowed-out cavity, almost able to picture the activity of everyday life that used to happen there.

I cross the street and walk past a patch of grass with shell cases sprouting up like gold metallic flowers—a semicircle of dried blood coats the cement in front of it. I get to the next street, and a massive crater stretches its width. It looks sketchy, so I reroute to the right hoping to circle around. My attention is fixed on the crater in awe that something was able to do that; I nearly trip over a pair of legs. I look down and see a haggard man sitting on the ground, his back against the wall. His jeans are in tatters, and stains line the fabric and stretch onto his t-shirt. A scraggly beard frames a broad grimy face. On the ground next to him is a red hat torn to shreds. It sits next to a jar with a few coins in it.

"Spare any change, brother?" the man says.

In his cracked, dirty hands is a sign with the words I was wrong scrawled out on it.

A spark of rage flares up inside me reading the sign. My fingers curl into fists at my side. I want to strangle the life out of this person I don't even know.

"A little late for that now, isn't it?" I say, nodding at his sign.

"I was lied to, brother."

"I don't believe that."

"Can you help me out here?"

"Is this what you wanted?" I ask, holding my arms out to the wounded city. "Was this worth it?"

"I'm trying to atone, brother."

I have the urge to punch him in his face, over and over again, but I resist. I've got a more important task at hand.

"Whatever," I say in disgust as I walk away. I hear the man shout after me.

"We can be whole again."

My blood boils as I storm up to the next street. I have nowhere to unleash my anger, so I let it implode in my chest. As I'm walking, a Leftie Humvee patrol rumbles past. A soldier with a protocol scanner passes the beam over me. My phone vibrates, and the authorization protocol pings as the beam confirms who I am. The Humvee continues. I need to get off the main roads. An alleyway is ten feet away. I cut down it, stopping in the shadows at the other end before emerging into the street. It's clear, so I keep going. A jet screams overhead. It's low, and the noise startles me into picking up the pace. Two more go by, and I hear gunfire in the distance. Then I hear a thump, thump, thump beating through the air. Helicopters.

Then more gunfire. Something is happening. Something big. I throw caution to the wind and break into a sprint for the three remaining blocks. A pair of Humvees blow by.

A stream of gunfire roars out not far from me. I duck into an alley and hide behind a Dumpster. Five Lefties march past. I count to ten, then run for it, committed to not stopping until I reach the pharmacy. Rounding the next corner, I see the store. It looks dark inside, and panic creeps up my neck. I race to the door and pull. It doesn't open, so I bang on the glass.

"Please. Is anyone there? Please open up," I shout.

Cupping my hands against the glass, I peer inside for any signs of life. I'm about to turn away when I spot movement. A head peeks over the top of the counter inside.

"Please," I shout again. "I just need this prescription filled." I fumble to get the paper out, then hold it against the glass. "It's for my wife. Please. She's pregnant."

The last part seems to tug at the humanity of whoever's inside. Slowly, the person comes out from around the counter. It's an older man dressed in a white pharmacist jacket with thick glasses and a bald patch extending to his sideburns. He's terrified but trying to hide it. He edges towards the door and steals a glance at the prescription. Then his eyes meet mine, studying them briefly, deciding if he will let me in.

I breathe and remove as much panic from my voice as possible.

"Please. These pills are for my wife. She's sick."

The pharmacist gives in and unlocks the doors.

"Hurry up and get in here," he says.

As soon as I'm in, he slams the door shut and locks it again.

"Thank you," I say.

"Come on, then, let's hurry this along."

I hand him the slip of paper, and he disappears behind

the counter. He returns a minute later with a bottle of pills.

"Here you go," he says.

"How much is it?"

"Just take it."

"Are you sure?"

"What's the difference at this point?"

I nod as I stuff the pills in my pocket and start for the door.

"I knew this was going to happen," the pharmacist says. "My son's out there, with the Left. A Captain."

The pharmacist comes around the counter to let me out.

"My son said the big one was coming soon, but they would have to do it without warning. Too many communications are getting hacked, I guess. Today's that day; it sounds like. Let's hope this ends it, so we can all move on."

"Here's hoping," I say.

He unlocks the door and steps aside. I tap the pills in my pocket.

"Thank you again."

He nods, "Good luck."

Another plane streaks above me as I come out of the store. I track it until I lose it behind a building. The ground shakes. Smoke is pouring over the skyline like waves over a breaker. The ground shakes again. Then again. The gray clouds are turning a hideous black as the smoke seeps in. Plumes rise into the air, seeming to surround the city. One section in particular, though, has a higher concentration. Then I realize where it is, and my body goes numb. Some sort of autopilot in my brain pushes me towards the smoke, directing me home.

The rumble of a collapsing building reverberates through my feet. The ground quakes again and again. The sound of gunfire comes in short bursts. A helicopter sweeps past, spitting a hail of bullets into a truck, perforating everyone inside. The truck careens into the side of a building, and the impact flings the riddled bodies from the bed. The sight barely registers. I'm too focused on getting back to Isla as fast as my legs will carry me. She's ok. She's ok. She has to be ok. They didn't use missiles. Those weren't missiles. They said they wouldn't use them. The ground shaking and the smoke, that's from... that's from...ah hell. I give up convincing myself of the lie I'm trying to tell. As I get closer, the thick smoke makes the air taste coarse and bitter.

I round the last corner and skid to a stop. My mind struggles to process what I'm seeing. Two blocks' worth of buildings are leveled, reduced to hills of crumbled brick, powdered cement, and twisted steel. The half-standing buildings are missing their outer walls like a cake with the edges cut away. Debris spills into the street in clumps. The landscape looks so foreign I question if I'm in the right spot. My brain tries to continue lying, that I'm somewhere else, that I am, in fact, in the wrong place. If I just look to my right, I'll see my apartment still intact and whole. My heart, though, accepts the reality of what I'm facing. My home is gone, and so is Isla, along with the child that I'll now never meet.

I stagger forward, not sure what else to do. Picking my way through the maze of destruction, I stop where my apartment once stood. Maybe she's still alive; my brain yells. I cling to the hopeless thought and scramble up the rubble, picking a random spot to dig with my hands. I dig and dig and dig until the pain becomes too great. Blood drips from my fingertips. I ignore it and try to lift a massive cement slab, but it doesn't budge. I try to scream Isla's name, but my throat is so choked by the dust in the air that nothing comes out. Keep going;

my brain goads me. Don't be weak. Don't give up. Find her.

I see a pile of smaller loose bricks. I stumble to them and start chucking them aside. Find her. More bricks. I scratch and claw, pull, and dig like a dog after a bone. Find her. I get down a foot into the debris when I hit a hunk of metal. I scoop my hands under it and lift. A muscle pops in my back, sending me to my knees.

"Find her," I mutter.

But I can't. Isla's gone. My heart and brain go silent as I collapse into the ruins of my life.

Chapter 4

A high-powered beam of light pries my eyes open. The light flicks away, and I hear a voice.

"Hey, we got a live one over here," the voice shouts.

Another voice replies, "Who're they with?"

"Let me check."

My eyes focus through the yellow splotches to see someone standing over me. It's dark, so I can't distinguish any features. A green beam emits from a scanner, covering my body until it registers who I am.

"He's with us. A civilian," the first voice shouts back.

"They need a medic?" the second voice says.

"Hang tight, let me see."

The flashlight is on again, and the guy crouches down. In the ambient light, I can tell he's a soldier.

"Hey, buddy, can you hear me?" he says.

I stare at him, not wanting to move, not wanting to speak, not wanting to do anything, but lay at this gravesite, this sacred site, until I'm with Isla again. The flashlight pans across my eyes when I don't respond.

The soldier shouts back to the second voice, "I think this guy's in shock. Better send a stretcher up."

"Roger that."

He looks back at me and pats my shoulder.

"We'll get you out of here. You're safe now," the soldier says.

Gravel crunches beneath boots approaching. I want to scream at them for trodding over my wife, disturbing her, but I can't say anything. No part of my body seems to work. It feels like someone filled me up with novocaine. The soldiers drop a stretcher by my side. Four hands grip me by my clothes and hoist me onto the stretcher. They jostle me around as they descend from the debris that once was my home. A door opens, and they load me into a military ambulance. It smells of death and despair. Someone new pops into my line of sight.

"What do we got?" the new guy asks.

"Not sure," the soldier who found me says. He's sitting on my right. "He hasn't said anything yet."

The new guy, a medic, I'm guessing, examines me. He squeezes and prods here and there, then gets to my hands.

"Jesus," the medic says, rotating my hands. He lifts them for the other soldier to see.

"Damn, the guy must have been digging. Probably lost someone in there? The scan said he lived in that grid. Guessing that was his apartment. Hey, buddy, was that your apartment?"

I don't answer.

"What's his name?" the medic asks.

The soldier references his scanner, "Says his name is

Ezra Asher."

"Ezra," the medic says. He's hovering over my face. His breath smells like wet coffee grounds. "Do you know where you are? Can you tell us what happened? Other than your hands, does anything else hurt?"

Hurt? I lost part of myself, part of my soul. There aren't enough words to describe the pain I feel. I reach for my back.

"You did something to your back?" the medic asks.

I nod. He rolls me on my side and lifts my shirt. His fingers probe for any serious damage; then, he eases me back.

"No wounds. I feel a little tightness. That's probably a pulled muscle. Any other pain?"

I shake my head no. The two men each take a hand and douse it with some liquid that burns like hell. Then they apply a thick layer of something that feels like jelly to my fingers and finish them off with bandages.

"Do you have any place to go? Any other friends or family," the medic says.

I shake my head and mumble.

"What's that?" he asks, leaning his ear towards my mouth.

"I couldn't...find her," I whisper. Saying the words out loud puts a finality onto Isla's and the baby's death. The last shreds of my dignity evaporate, and I break down sobbing. Tears mixing with the dirt create a mudslide of sorrow down the slope of my face. I close my eyes, trying to control the spasms from the sobbing, but I can't. I failed them. If I hadn't left, I would be with them right now instead of being stranded in this desolate hell.

The men with me are quiet as I get myself together. When my body stops shaking, the medic puts his hand on my shoulder.

"I'm going to give you a little something for the pain," he says.

A needle pricks my vein in the crook of my arm. My blood turns warm as the contents of the shot flood my system.

"Let's bring him to Safety Zone F," the medic says to the soldier. "They should be able to take care of him there. He's going to need one of the head benders more than anything."

"Yeah, for sure," the soldier says. "I'll write it up now in his file. Poor bastard."

It's the last thing I hear before I succumb to the warmth of darkness.

WEEK 8 - NOVEMBER 7

I wake up to a cool breeze licking my fingers. My eyes open. I'm staring at a tall ceiling that seems to go on for miles. I'm lying down on something uncomfortable. It's low to the ground. A cot, maybe. Soft skin trickles over the palm of my hand. I sit up and see a woman seated next to me. She's in her late forties and is rather beautiful. A white cap perches atop a head of platinum blonde hair ironed board straight, stopping an inch before her shoulders. The white kimono-inspired shirt that is standard attire for a Redeemer hugs the curves of her toned body. I'd heard of people in the Redeemer program but had yet to meet one. The Redeemers were formed years ago as a sort of Peace Corp for the underprivileged but funded by the city's wealthy elite as an alternate form of taxation. The woman has inviting eyes and smiles at me with thin lips.

"I'm sorry. I didn't mean to wake you," she says. "Your fingers are healing up quite nicely. I thought some air on them would feel nice."

I glance at my hands and see hardening scabs along each fingertip. Flexing the joints is uncomfortable, but overall there isn't much pain. Someone replaced the clothes I had on when the soldiers found me. I've got on navy blue linen pants with a matching button-up shirt over a gray t-shirt. Thick gray socks cover my feet. I survey the space I'm in. Four walls of thick tan canvas box me in. Each wall suspends from thick tubing eight feet in the air. Where the walls meet, the fabric is zip tied to vertical tubes. The door area has the canvas divided down the middle with a zipper, similar to a tent. Aside from the cot and the stool the nurse is sitting on, the only other object in the room is a compact nightstand with a single large drawer. Ambient sounds of a crowd seep in through the fabric.

"Where am I?" I ask.

"You're in Safety Zone F," she replies. "You were brought in four days ago."

"I've been out for four days?"

"More or less, yes. We gave you sedatives to allow your hands to heal."

"I'm in the stadium?"

"That's right. The government converted it early on in the conflict."

"What's your name?"

"I'm Skylar Moore. You can just call me Skylar."

She rises gracefully from the stool and lifts her tablet from the nightstand.

"It's good to hear you talking," she says as she focuses on the screen. "Your file says you suffered mild shock when the soldiers found you. Your fingers have healed to a sufficient stage where I don't believe bandages are required any longer. How is your back feeling?"

I massage the spot and slowly twist my torso, waiting for any shooting pain.

"It's fine."

"Excellent," she says, typing a note on the tablet. She resumes her spot on the stool and rests the device on her lap. Her eyes soften as she peers into mine.

"There are a few things I need to cover with you. Some of this might be...challenging, but I'm required to review it. After that, I'll leave you to yourself."

"Ok," I say, a bit uneasy about what she has to go over.

"It has been confirmed that your primary residence has been rendered unlivable. Your records show you have no, ah-hem, excuse me, no remaining family."

Her eye contact breaks from mine as she says the words. She squints at the tablet, composing herself before continuing.

"In your circumstances, you are allowed two weeks to stay here in the Safety Zone facilities, during which time you can seek other living arrangements. If you cannot find them on your own in the two weeks, then the city will relocate you to a facility for the displaced. You will then have four weeks there to find a more permanent residence. If you are unable to, then you can apply for semi-permanent residence status, which in your case, shouldn't be a problem getting. With that status, the city gives you six months to find a new home. Do you understand what I've just told you?"

I nod.

"Ok, then please imprint here," she says, then holds the tablet towards me. I place my thumb on the screen, the least damaged of my fingers. The device turns green from a successful scan, and she takes the tablet back.

"Next, we'll cover employment."

"Wait," I say, rubbing my eyebrows. "I'm sorry, but what about the fighting?"

"Oh, yes, of course. How foolish of me. I forget you have

been out of things for a few days." Her face brightens. "The siege four days ago was a success. The Left now controls ninety-seven percent of the city. The remainder of the holdouts are predicted to be cleared out by the end of the week."

"What are you saying?"

"There's nothing official yet, but it seems the Left has won. The war, at least here anyway, is over."

I roll her words over in my head, 'The siege four days ago was a success.' A success. For who? For me, the cost of that success was too steep a price.

"I see."

"Anyway," Skylar continues. "As I was saying, now we can discuss employment. Your file shows you worked in the solar field."

"That's right."

"It will be up to your employer's discretion as to your employment status. The time frame for employment follows the same schedule as the timeframe for finding a new residence. If you can't find a job or return to your old one, then you can work with any of the crews to clean up the city. Those jobs will be in high demand."

She says this last part with too much enthusiasm and realizes how it came across. Her jaw clenches tight, then relaxes.

"I apologize. That came out wrong. I wasn't thinking."

"It's ok," I say.

She forces a tiny smile and nods.

"So you understand everything I told you for employment?"

"Yes."

"Then please imprint here."

I scan my thumb again; then, she studies the screen a little too long. There's something else.

"The medic that brought you in also flagged you for needing a mental evaluation. So you'll need to speak with someone from the Mental Health Division before you can leave here."

"Is that necessary?"

"The mental health of all the city's citizens is vital to peace."

"That's rich," I sneer. "You actually believe that crap?"

"It's just talking."

"Yeah, and if one of those head benders thinks I'm a danger to society, they'll lock me away for the rest of my life."

A decade ago, mental health initiatives were a big push for the Left's political platforms. They wanted to create an easily accessible means for people to seek help. The idea was good in theory, but a shortage of finding qualified candidates for the jobs through a wrench in things. The pay was also terrible, the hours were grueling, and the day-to-day topics weren't exactly the easiest to deal with. So, they turned to A.I. robots again, similar to TURING. I don't even remember the actual name of the robotic therapists. Everyone refers to them as head benders since the device attaches to your head. I've never used one, but from what I'm told, it's quite the experience. In the early days of their implementation, some people went insane after using it, while others committed suicide. The courts started allowing their data as evidence in trials, which led to multiple wrongful convictions and sent people to asylums. Most of these flaws got ironed out over the years, but the early issues created a stigma and fear of the head benders. A fear I hold myself.

"I'm ok. I'm fine now," I plead with Skylar. "That was just...it was a tough day. You know? You can't remove that part from my file?"

"I'm sorry, that's above my authorization level."

I sigh, "Ok."

"Would you like to schedule your appointment now?"

"Might as well. I'll take whatever the soonest available is. Get it over with."

She taps on the tablet, scrolling through appointment slots.

"There's one available at six tonight. Does that work?"

I shrug, "Fine."

"Alright, I have you scheduled at six o'clock with Dr. Walton. The appointment details are now available in the city app. Do you have any questions before I go?"

"Can I leave this room?"

"Yes, you have free range of the stadium. If you leave this room, it will lock behind you. You can get back in with your imprint scan. You can also use the restrooms or schedule a time for a shower in one of the locker rooms through the app."

"Can I leave the Safety Zone?"

She fidgets with the tablet and says, "Well, to put it bluntly, no. Not until Dr. Walton administers his mental evaluation. I'm sorry."

"So I'm a prisoner?"

She frowns, "No. You're not a prisoner. It's just routine for keeping yourself and the greater good safe."

"Is it?"

"I don't make the rules, Mr. Asher."

Skylar stands from the stool and smooths out her uniform with her free hand. She points to the nightstand.

"Your personal effects are in the drawer. We disposed of the clothes you were wearing. You'll also find a daily allotment of painkillers for your injuries. You have a pair of shoes at the foot of the bed."

She moves to the door and unzips it, then glances over her shoulder.

"If you need any other assistance, you can message me through your phone."

I nod, and she zips the door and is gone. I pause a moment before putting my feet on the highly polished floor. My muscles ache but loosen a little after I stretch each of them. I put my thumb on the nightstand scanner glass, and the drawer pops open with a soft hiss. Inside is my phone, my Leatherman, which I'm surprised they let me keep, keys, and the packet of painkillers. I stuff everything but the pills in my pockets, holding them for a moment. My eyes close as I picture Isla at her best, but all I visualize is her buried beneath the weight of a building. She must have been so scared. And I wasn't there to protect her. Tears well in my eyes. I toss the pills back in the drawer and close it. I haven't earned the right to be pain-free.

The provided shoes are where Skylar said they'd be. They're low-top gray canvas slide-ons. An urge to get out of the confined space overcomes me. I shove my feet into the shoes, then fumble with the zipper on the door. As I close the flaps, an overhead sensor chimes, locking the room behind me. The time on my phone says it's four forty-five, leaving me just over an hour before my appointment. I figure I'll kill some time exploring.

Ten years ago, the city built the stadium for basketball. It was one of the few things the Left and Right could agree on at the time. The team, though, was terrible. In their ten-year run, they never once made it to the playoffs. So the goodwill intended to bring the two sides together furthered the divide. Each side blamed the other for the misuse of taxpayers' dollars.

The court floor splits into four quadrants of identical makeshift rooms like mine. Nurses are coming in and out at a steady pace. I head left down the center aisle until I reach the intersection, then take another left, heading into the stands.

Families huddle together in their seats, eating rations out of pouches. Others dressed like me are sitting alone, staring at the court as if a game will start any second. I climb the stairs and head for one of the entryways leading to the outer corridors surrounding the court. More of the makeshift rooms line the near wall of the corridor. The opposite wall has a mix of booths set up at intervals. Some are food stands left over from before the war, and others are general services. I pass a milkshake stand, then an eye doctor, a dentist, and even a barber. The smell of chicken wings catches my attention, and I realize how hungry I am. Fifty feet later, I find the stand. I check my phone and see I still have a little left in my bank account. I order fourteen wings and a large lemonade. The guy operating the register hands me a styrofoam box with the wings, and I shuffle along, stopping at an empty bench.

I break into the wings. They've got a nice heat, and I polish them off like a rabid dog. I down half the lemonade and then wipe my hands with a wet wipe. I think about some of the information that Skylar told me. I haven't worked in close to two months. I figure that's an easy enough place to start. Maybe if I throw myself into work, I can distract my mind from drifting to Isla. I find my boss's number and listen as the other line rings. An unfamiliar voice answers.

"This is Agent Maleev," the voice says.

"Oh, I'm sorry. I must have dialed the wrong number."

"You were looking for Jim Deakins, correct?"

"Yes, that's right."

"I regret to inform you that Mr. Deakins has been killed."

"Really. What...what happened?"

"I'm not at liberty to say much, but he failed to pass the authorization protocol. He is under investigation for ties with the Right."

"Jesus," I murmur.

"I see from your number that you're Ezra Asher, yes?"

My palms are sweating. Deakins had ties to the Right? I would've never taken him for being on their side. And now he's dead, and some agent is answering his phone?

I hesitate, then say, "Yes. That's me. I was just calling to see about starting up work again."

"I'm sorry, but that won't be possible. Mr. Deakins' accounts and business dealings are part of the investigation. Helios Solar as you knew it no longer exists."

"Oh, ok."

"I wish I had better news for you. If we need you for questioning, we'll contact you. Goodbye."

The line goes dead. I slip the phone back into my pocket, dazed by the call. My stomach twists, and I feel like I'm going to vomit. I walk briskly, trying to tamp down the bile. I can't keep it down and have to settle for puking in a trash can. In hindsight, wings probably weren't the best choice for my first meal in days. A few people walking by give me dirty looks. I continue through the corridor and find the restrooms. At the farthest sink, a guy is shaving. He throws me a glance, then resumes his shave. I gargle water, getting the taste of the regurgitated wings out of my mouth. The mirror highlights the paleness of my skin. I suddenly feel as tired as I look. After taking a piss, I return to the corridor. The grogginess that has settled over me reduces my desire to explore further.

I take out my phone and follow the map to the head bender's office. The walk takes me ten minutes. His office is in the lower levels of the stadiums where he's commandeered a coach's office. An imprint screen with a registration sign is on a stand by the door. Five plastic chairs rest against the wall. A woman sits on one with her head tilted back, resting it against the wall. Her eyes are closed, and she doesn't open them when I sit down two chairs over. I find myself matching her pose. When did I get so damn tired? Exhaustion carries me between the gray spaces of sleep and reality. In a useless attempt, I still try to ignore the tightness in my stomach. The light gets darker behind my eyelids. Someone is standing in front of me.

"Mr. Asher."

I open my eyes to see a round woman with short gray hair wearing sleek clear glasses. I sit up straighter in the chair.

"That's me," I say.

"Dr. Walton is ready for you."

I notice the other waiting woman is gone. The round woman moves to the door and holds her arm out for me to go in first. A computer sits on a desk in a small alcove. Three doors span the remainder of the office. She settles in behind me, then points to the middle door, the only one open.

"He's in room two," she says.

I inch towards the door and peek in. Walton is sitting behind a desk. He's a slender black guy with a shaved head, and a goatee headed to white. Aviator-style glasses perch on his nose. He spots me, so I force myself into the room.

"You must be Mr. Asher," he says, standing from his seat and motioning for me to sit down. "Is it alright if I call you Ezra?"

"Sure."

"Perfect."

Walton props a tablet on the desk, presses a button, and the door closes behind me. He then opens a metal case about the size of a 12-pack of beer. From it, he takes out a pair of virtual reality-inspired goggles. They're white with a random collection of dangling wires.

"Have you ever used one of these before?" Dr. Walton says. I shake my head.

"All right, well, they're pretty straightforward. Nothing to be concerned about. I'll slide this over your head, and two probes will attach to your temples. You can insert the earbuds after I put this on you."

He hands me a pair of white earbuds.

"Once the program is activated, you'll respond to what you see and hear. I'll be outside monitoring your progress. If there are any issues, press this button."

Out of the case, he hands me a small white remote with a single button.

"Just know pressing the button doesn't automatically cancel the session. That is left to my discretion. Do you understand?"

I nod.

"Ok, then let's get started," he says.

Dr. Walton places the set over my head and centers it over my eyes. Then he attaches the probes to my temples.

"You can put the earbuds in now," he says. "Once they're in, I'll leave the room, and your session will begin."

I put the earbuds in, then hear the door open and close. I'm nervous. Going into the unknown and what this computer will expose about myself terrifies me. The visuals in the goggles go dark, then a gradient of oranges and yellows fills the screen. A circle spins in the center with my name on the screen and the words, analyzing. Once it has finished, sounds of nature come in through the earbuds, and visuals of a forest appear on the screen. I'm amazed at how lifelike the experience is. A man walks out from behind a tree. He's dressed in a brown tweed three-piece suit. There's something familiar about him, and then I realize he's an actor I like, and that makes me realize just how sophisticated and how much these robots know about us. I also love forests, so they must have accessed that in my records. Why? Maybe to get the dopamine going and put me at ease?

"Hello," the man says. "You may call me Michael."

When I don't respond, Michael turns and gives me a gentle wave. "Walk with me," he says.

The whole setup is weird to me, yet, I feel like I'm really there with him, and part of me finds it can't resist. My mind propels me forward.

"So, Ezra, I understand you've suffered a great loss recently."

I nod and see the ground go up and down as if I were there.

"Why don't you tell me what happened?"

"It's not all there in my file?"

"Yes, most of it is," Michael says, giving me a disarming smile. "But that only gives me surface details. I want to know you. I want to go below the surface."

I don't respond. Below the surface is the last place I want to go. I rub the scabs on my fingers, trying to control my heartbeat.

"Why don't we start at the beginning," Michael says. "The medics that found you said you were sleeping on top of the rubble of a building. Why was that?"

"You already know that."

"You don't have to be afraid, Ezra," Michael says. "It was your home, yes?"

I don't say anything.

"And what happened there?"

"I think that's pretty clear."

"The medics said you wouldn't talk when they found you, but you did say...." Michael stops walking and looks at me. "'I couldn't find her.' Then you burst into tears. Who couldn't you find?"

"Why are you doing this?"

"We need to acknowledge what happened. You won't be able to move on until you do that."

I consider pressing the button in my hand. I want to rip this stupid device off my head and run out of the room. But where would that get me? A life in a straightjacket?

"Who couldn't you find?" Michael repeats.

"My wife."

"What was her name?"

"Isla."

"Isla. That's a beautiful name. Why don't you tell me a little about her?"

"Like what?"

"How did you meet?"

I think back to when we were eighteen. Suddenly, the visuals in front of me jump to a beach. A young Isla stands there wearing an orange vest, holding a garbage bag. Other teenagers surround her.

"What is this?" I say, startled.

"This is your memory brought to life," Michael says, surveying the scene next to me on the beach.

"I...I don't like this."

"It's ok. Just breathe and take me through what we're seeing."

Sounds of the ocean come through the earbuds. I can almost taste the salty air.

"We were cleaning up at the beach for community service hours we were required to complete."

"Court mandated, your records show. What did you do?"

"I crashed my dad's car into a fire hydrant. She got nabbed

for being drunk and spray painting Fuck You on the side of her high school."

"Go ahead," Michael says, walking around Isla.

"It was stupid. I was stupid. I took my dad's car when I wasn't supposed to. I just wanted attention. I wanted my parents to notice me for once, even if it was for doing something wrong."

"Why didn't they notice you?"

"I...I had an older sister...she died young from a rare cancer. I was young when she died, so I didn't really know her. My parents... just couldn't move past her death. I was there, but all they wanted to see was her."

"That must have been hard."

"I made my peace with it."

"And what about your wife?"

"Her dad apparently led a secret life. He started another family with another woman and eventually left Isla and her mom. The incident at the school happened shortly after her dad left."

"That drew you together?"

"Yes. We never left each other's side after that."

I smile as I watch the young Isla glide over the sand. The memory seems like a lifetime ago.

"And tell me about the child?"

"What did you say to me?"

"Recent records show you hired Dr. Powell for a pregnancy consultation. Was your wife expecting?"

"You shouldn't know that. That's... that's not for you to know."

"Did you always want children?"

"Why are you doing this?"

"It's a simple question."

"Isla always wanted a big family. I vowed my life to her to

give her everything she wanted."

"You didn't quite answer the question. I asked about you."

"I don't know."

Michael comes to my side, listening intently without judgment.

"It's alright," he says.

"I was afraid I'd turn out like my parents. Part of me was relieved when she had the miscarriages. The other part of me, though, looked forward to not being them. And giving a child an upbringing that was better than mine." I stare at the young Isla as the waves part around her ankles. "I wanted to love a child the way I never was."

Michael looks at me, his eyes lined with sympathy. I would hug him if he were real. Instead, I'm embraced by loneliness.

"Are you ready to tell me what happened next?" Michael says. The beach fades away, and we're back in the forest.

"What happened to Isla?"

It's a struggle to talk. My throat feels two sizes too small.

"There were...bombs...an attack...."

"What were you doing when these bombs hit?"

"I was getting medicine," I mumble. "Isla was sick."

"And this makes you feel guilty?"

I nod. The tears bang on the base of my eyeballs like angry hordes trying to break down a castle gate.

"I shouldn't have left her," I say.

"You were trying to help her. We, unfortunately, can control very little in our lives. Chance changed your life. You're not to blame for that."

We emerge to an open patch in front of an expansive lake. Michael sits down on a rock.

"I didn't get to say goodbye," I say, sitting next to him. "I didn't know...that was going to be the last...." The words choke off. I shake my head, "I was cheated from something so simple. And now I have nothing and no one. No job. No money. No place to live. The only thing that surrounds me is death."

"You feel hopeless?"

The tears force their way through and trickle down my face. I wipe the remnants that have escaped from the headset from my cheeks with my palm.

"Please," I say. "Just fucking stop."

"Anger is good," Michael says, unphased by my cursing. "It's a sign you're not completely lost from coming back."

"Coming back? How do I come back from this?" I ask, staring into his eyes for the first time, pleading that he can give me the answers to make the pain disappear.

"Only time can answer that question, I'm afraid. The more living you do, the more likely you'll find the path. You are grieving, which is normal and understandable given your circumstances." Michael pauses until I focus on him. "One day, you'll find your way out from the ruins. You'll see."

A robin lands on a rock next to me, tweets a short little song, and then flies off. When I look back, Michael's gone. The forest fades away and goes black. I hear the door open behind me and then feel Dr. Walton removing the probes from my temples. I take out the earbuds and wait for the headset to come off. Once it does, I see Dr. Walton quietly studying me. He rubs his goatee, then ambles over to a machine on the edge of his desk. After tapping a few buttons on the tablet, the machine beeps, coming to life. The machine beeps again, and a handful of pills fall into a small white envelope. The envelope drops into a tray at the base of the machine. Walton grabs the envelope, peels off the backing of an adhesive strip, and folds it shut. He then hovers his tablet camera over the barcode printed on the envelope.

"These pills should help with what you're feeling. Take two a day, and you'll see things in a new light," Walton says, passing me the pills.

I slip them into my pocket and struggle to stand. I can barely keep my eyes open. The energy drained from my body.

"I'll mark your file as cleared, but I'm recommending a monthly check-in for the next six months. Please don't make me regret this decision," Dr. Walton says, holding his hand for me to shake. I take his hand, and he grips mine as a father might before imparting a pearl of wisdom. But he doesn't say anything.

He lets go of my hand, and I stumble out. Getting back to my assigned room on the court passes in a blur. I'm not even sure how I managed to find it. Sitting on the lip of the cot, I remove the pills from my pocket. I stare at them for a long time, debating whether to take them. Two minutes later, I scan my thumb, and the nightstand drawer pops open. I toss the packet of pills in and close the drawer. I slip my feet out of the shoes and curl up on the cot, with the taste of salt air lingering against my tongue.

Chapter 5

The remainder of my time at the stadium goes by in a haze. I sleep most of the days, only getting up to go to the bathroom and drink a meal replacement shake. The shakes are bland, but I'm not drinking them for taste. They keep me alive for the time being. I went three days without eating, thinking I could starve myself to death. The resulting agonizing pain in my stomach was too much, so I gave up. I'm not afraid of suffering. Hell, that's all I've been doing lately, but starvation is too much work. From all the survival shows I watched, the hosts would say you could go three weeks without eating. That's too drawn out for me. I exist, but I'm not living—a coward, unable to commit. When my two weeks are up, a nurse comes to get me. She performs a final exam to add to my file. I've lost fifteen pounds and haven't shaved or taken a shower since I arrived. The concern on the nurse's face is clear as day, but she signs me out anyway. They need the beds.

Someone directs me to a line for the people departing. I shuffle along with the rest of the lost souls, and we get loaded onto a school bus. A guy who smells just as rank as I do slumps into the seat with me. Gauze weaves around his forearms down to his wrists. He tried opening his veins, is my guess. I think about going that way, and it makes me lightheaded. Too grisly. The ride is slow and bumpy. Many streets remain blocked with debris that forces the buses to reroute multiple times to get to our destination. The bus stops forty minutes later outside a worn-out eight-story building.

As I descend the bus's stairs, I recognize where we are—about six blocks from where I used to live. The gridded map comes to mind. We're somewhere around grid square 8-4. From what I remember, the Right used to control this section heavily. The building is a gray rectangle that runs five sets of windows wide by three sets deep. Small concrete balconies jut out from each room. At the head of the group is a tall woman. She's corralling us together.

"Alright, everyone, please listen up," she shouts so people in the back can hear her. "This is your new home for the next four weeks. We posted room assignments on your phones. The property owners converted the first floor into a mess hall. Meals will be provided for you twice daily. The schedule and menu also live on your phone. It should have been explained to you at the Safety Zone. You have four weeks to find more permanent living arrangements. If you cannot, then it is recommended that you apply for an extension during the start of your fourth week here. If you get denied, then you will have to leave. I'll be here on the first floor for the next hour while you settle in. If there are any questions during that time, please don't hesitate to reach out."

She smiles and gives a wave for the group to follow her. The woman is up the steps in two long strides and into the building. I check my phone and see I'm in room 5c on the fifth floor. People are piling into the elevator, so I find the stairs. The lack of food and exercise makes climbing the stairs feel like I'm scaling Everest. Each step, I have to will my knees to bend. Others brush past me, eager to be somewhere new and out of the stadium. No one says anything to me, not that I would engage them back. Once I reach the fifth floor, I rest on the top steps, catching my breath. I wrangle my breathing to a normal level and exit the stairwell. I roam the hallways, stopping at my room. My thumb presses into the scanner, and the bolt unlocks.

I enter a studio apartment that's maybe three hundred square feet. It's one of the relatively new buildings, which means the architects designed every room to be as compact and space efficient as possible. As I walk in, there is a narrow hallway. One door is on the right wall that leads into the bathroom. The white tiled walls enclose a skinny shower, sink, and toilet. From the hallway, the room opens into the main space. Against the nearest wall stands a matte black counter with a sink next to a stove. Cabinets stretch above it to the ceiling. Beneath the counter is a small fridge to the right of the sink. Near the stove, an island extends into the room that serves as a table. Against the opposite wall is a fabric loveseat in matching matte black. The third wall has a floor-to-ceiling sliding door leading to the concrete balcony. Following this wall opens into the final segmented area, with a simple wood-framed twin bed, night-stand, and closet. A single window looks over the city on the same wall as the slider. Unpacking is easy since I came with nothing. I remove my shoes and collapse into the loveseat. The natural light seeping into the room lulls me into a deep sleep.

A car horn wakes me hours later. The room is dark, aside from the amber glow from the street lights. I'm startled by the unfamiliar setting until I remember where I am. With my hands in front of me, I inch towards the hallway and find the light switch. A soft white light gradually comes to life. I search the cabinets. All of them are empty except one that holds two glasses, two coffee mugs, two plates with utensils, and a small pot. I snatch a glass, fill it with water from the kitchen sink, and make my way out to the balcony.

The cool air brushes against my face as I move to the edge. The city is quiet as if in mourning. It seems to be trying hard to erase the cacophony of bullets and bombs that held it captive these last few months. Some of the windows have lights on in the building across the street. Are families in those rooms embracing each other, counting their blessings they survived this ordeal? Watching TV in the comfort of their own home and possessions while the rest of us attempt to figure out what to do next?

I sip the water and glance at the deserted street. Five floors up. That would do the trick, I imagine. I rest my forearms on the balcony rail, then let the glass slip from my hands, tracking its descent. It connects with the pavement and erupts into a million pieces. The smashing sound cements an exit plan in my head. Now I need to build the courage to see it through.

WEEK 10 - NOVEMBER 21

A knock comes at my door two days later. I open it, and standing in the hallway is Coop. He smiles, revealing the familiar black space of his missing tooth. His hair has grown out, and patches of stubble cover his face. He looks tired, but his eyes are the same, friendly and warm. A brown bag rests by his side. Before I can move or say anything, his arm shoots out, and he pulls me into a bear hug. For a minute, I can't distinguish if I'm imagining him being here.

"I can't believe you're alive," he says, breaking from the hug and looking me over.

"What are you...what are you doing here?"

He chuckles and slaps me in the chest with the back of his hand. "You invited me."

"I did?"

I don't remember any of this. My thoughts are blurry, and I can't place the memory of texting him. Maybe when I was on the balcony feeling lonely, I messaged him.

"I'd say you look good, but I'd be lying," he grins.

I put a hand to my face, feeling the coarse beard, realizing for the first time it's there. I'm still wearing the same clothes from the stadium.

"You going to let me in?" he asks.

I move aside and close the door once he's passed me. Coop strolls into the kitchen area and puts the brown bag on the island.

"So what're you doing here?" he asks. "Where's Isla?"

I shrug and mumble, "Dead."

"What?"

The levity drains from Coop's face.

"What happened?"

"A missile strike. A bomb. Who knows. Leveled the whole building with her in it."

He stares at me, his mouth ajar. I stare back, feeling nothing. The words may as well have come from a robot.

"When did this happen?" he says, sitting down on a stool

at the island.

"Three weeks ago, maybe."

"Wow, man. I'm sorry. Jesus. I don't even know what to say." He shakes his head, searching for the next question. "So, where have you been? Were you at one of the Safety Zones?"

I nod.

"And that's what you're doing here now?"

I nod again.

"Shit. I brought these beers thinking we would celebrate having made it through. Guess we're drinking for a different reason now."

Coop pulls a twelve-pack of beers out of the bag and places it on the island. He peels open the carton, removes two cans, cracks them open, then walks over to me. I take the cold can and put it to my lips absentmindedly. Coop does the same, downing half of it in the first go. I sit on the loveseat, and Coop parks himself on the stool.

"How about you? How is the family?" I ask him. Today is the most I've spoken in weeks.

Coop shrugs. I can tell that now that he knows what happened to Isla, he doesn't want to talk about his family.

"They're good, you know? It was tough while things were happening, and it's still a little uncertain where things will go. Most of the military has already pulled out of here."

"Really?"

"You didn't hear about any of this?"

I don't respond, staring at the mouth of the beer can.

"Yeah, so the Left is chasing the insurgents that fled the city. Guess battles are breaking out farther south too, so they're redirecting forces down there. The news said FEMA is supposed to come to help us out, but no one is hopeful that's going to happen. It seems the city is on its own for the time being."

I take another sip of the beer. It makes me feel nauseous, but each swig relaxes me a little. Coop finishes his can and opens another. He motions to the slider door.

"You mind if we get some air?" he says.

I tip my beer can toward the door. Coop helps me up from the loveseat, and we move to the balcony. I watch as he surveys the city, drinking his beer. Neither of us talks for a while. I nestle into the corner. I'm halfway through the beer, and I feel like I've had six. Without looking at me, Coop says, "I wish I knew you were going through all this. I'm sorry I wasn't there for you sooner. I'm heartbroken for you, man. I mean, how are you holding up?"

My appearance tells most of the story, but I think about the question. I haven't talked to anyone since the head bender. Another sip of beer goes down, and I gaze past Coop.

"I've been having this dream lately," I say. "I'm standing next to Isla when this missile comes through the ceiling. It's all in slow motion. She's not scared. She's just kind of there with this serene smile like it's no big deal. Her head bends up. The tip of the missile kisses her lips, and a white light fills the room. Then I watch as her body separates into tiny little bits. Then those bits keep breaking down until they're particles, like dust suspended in the air. In the dream, I walk into that dust, into her, and that's when I wake up. Now, whenever I'm outside, I like to take a deep breath and imagine I'm breathing her in. Bringing some part of her back to me."

Coop nods, then sighs, "That's rough. I can only imagine."

I pick at the pull tab on the can. "Isla was pregnant, too."

"What, in the dream?"

"No. We were going to have a kid."

For a second, Coop looks like he might be sick. He's shaking his head, about to say something, then stops. Coop steps back from the rail and leans against the building.

"Why didn't you tell me?"

"This is the first I've seen you."

"I mean that she was pregnant."

"Oh," I say. "I guess I didn't want to jinx it. A lot of good that did me."

Pain creases Coop's face in disbelief. He can't stop shaking his head, as if he shakes it enough, the words I've spoken will fall out.

"Was there...was there a funeral?" he asks.

"No. I don't know if anyone even found her body or if there's a body to find."

"God damn, Ezra. I'm so sorry, man." Coop rubs the back of his neck, at a loss for what to do or say. "Is there anything I can do?"

It's my turn to shake my head.

"You must've pissed off a karma god somewhere," Coop says. He slouches in defeat before finishing his second beer.

A sensation comes over me. One I haven't felt in a long time, and I can't help but laugh. It's a deep laugh that hurts my stomach. Coop frowns at my amusement with his comment that he didn't intend to be funny. Tears squeeze from the corner of my eyes. It's part hysterics and part relief.

"You want another?" Coop says, holding up his empty beer can.

I get myself under control and wipe the tears from my eyes. Coop disappears inside without getting an answer and comes out with two more beers he keeps for himself. The bit of laughter leaves me drained. I sit down and rest my wrists over my bent knees. Coop leans against the rail, still visibly rattled by my news, so I change the subject.

"Did you hear about Deakins?" I say.

"I heard."

"Did you know that about him?"

"I had my suspicions that he leaned to the Right, but I didn't think he leaned that far to get himself killed."

"Are you working?"

"I clean up debris during the day and then do odd jobs at night as an electrician. It doesn't pay as much as the larger city contracts we were doing, but it gets us by." Coop slugs back more beer. He looks at me then and says, "You should come with me tomorrow. Work a site with me. You can get some exercise. It'll get you out of the house. Take your mind off things."

I shrug, "I don't know."

"Come on. I miss working with you. At least give it a try. The city needs people. You show up, and you're hired."

He's convincing, but I'm uncertain if I'm in any shape to do it. I've let myself go with a specific endgame in mind. I know he's trying to be a good friend and wants to help, but would this just delay the inevitable? I don't think I'm ready for it. Before I can object to Coop's request, he says, "I'll be here tomorrow morning at nine. I'll bring breakfast. I know a guy that's been able to get us some decent food. It costs a fucking fortune, but it's better than eating that powder ration crap the food banks hand out."

I humor him and say, "Ok." I can give him a day. For his friendship, I owe him that, at least.

WEEK 10 - NOVEMBER 22

True to his word, Coop is at my door the next morning with breakfast. Another brown paper bag is in his left hand, and a canvas tote is in the other. A black pack is on his back. He sits at the island, places two sandwiches wrapped in greasy parchment paper on napkins, and slides one over to me with a black coffee.

"Savor this," he says. "You know how hard it is to get eggs these days."

I unwrap the paper. Between two slices of dry bread are hard-boiled eggs sliced into rings. Salt and pepper season the eggs; they're still warm as I take the first bite. I chew each bite slowly, waiting a few seconds to make sure they won't come back up before eating another piece. The coffee is weak and tastes a few days old, but it's hot and helps me wake up. Coop nods at the canvas tote.

"I brought you some boots and spare clothes. Figured you might need them."

"Thanks."

"No problem," he says between bites. He wolfs down the rest of the sandwich and drains his coffee. "Come on, eat up. We should get moving."

I wrap the remainder of the sandwich and drink the coffee. "I'll take the rest with me."

Coop hands me the canvas tote, and I go into the bedroom. Inside the tote are three sets of neatly folded jeans, flannel button-downs, socks and underwear, and a pair of work boots. The generosity almost brings me to tears. I strip naked, get dressed in fresh clothes, and then head to the kitchen.

"Ah, good. I'm glad it fits," Coop says. "Ready?"

I don't feel ready, but I nod that I am and follow him out

of the building. On the street, I search for Coop's car.

"Where'd you park?" I ask.

"Eh, I sold it," he says. "Needed the money. Besides, half the roads are cluttered with shit. It wasn't worth keeping around. I mostly walk places now. We've got a bike with a basket if we need to cart stuff around for longer distances."

"I'm sorry to hear that. I know you loved that car more than some of your kids."

He grins. "Yeah, well, what are you going to do? Honestly, I don't miss it that much."

"Where are we off to?"

Coop checks his phone and says, "Looks like they need people at grid 6-3."

We walk north. Two blocks in, and I have to ask Coop to slow down.

"Sorry," he says. "Don't worry. This job will whip you into shape. Christ, it feels good to be outside again. I don't know about you, but I was going out of my mind trapped inside for so long. I felt so useless and aimless. Never thought about what it'd be like not working and how much doing something does for you."

"This gives you that?"

"To a certain extent. I didn't think I'd be starting over at this point in my life, but it feels good to be doing something. Even if that's moving a brick from point A to point B."

We pass a block that on the right is pristine, but just across the street, it's blown to hell. The juxtaposition of it is surreal.

"Is the whole city like this?" I ask.

"Some decent pockets of it for sure. So much for not using bombs, huh? I don't know why I'm still surprised by politicians."

"And food is hard to come by?"

"It's starting to get better. Supply chain and all that is slowing things down. Most other cities are going through this too. You never know what you'll get for roads, so everything takes longer."

On the next block, two men are painting the side of the building. Glass from the first-floor windows lies on the ground, but the rest of the building is intact. The men's rollers cover a red R spray painted on the bricks.

"You think any of them are still around?" I say.

"Insurgents? Yeah, there's probably some hiding out around here. I don't think anyone realized how many of them were here. The Left killed a ton of them, that's for sure."

The mention of death makes Coop scratch the back of his head. I can tell he's trying not to trigger me.

"Do you need to rest?" he asks.

"I'm alright."

Another block, and we're there. The weapons of war left their marks on the street. Rubble fills the entirety of the pavement. About twenty people are already working, holding whatever they can carry and lugging it to one of five dump trucks scattered at the street's entrance. Coop approaches a black guy holding a tablet and wearing a hard hat.

"Zeke, how're you doing?" Coop says.

Zeke turns and smiles when he recognizes Coop. They shake hands.

"I got us another recruit."

Coop claps his hand on my shoulder. Zeke studies me with doubt.

"Jesus," Zeke says. "Where'd you find him? A Dumpster?"

"Beggars can't be choosers."

"Thanks for the vote of confidence," I say.

Coop and Zeke laugh at this.

"You got a name?" Zeke asks.

"Ezra," I say as we shake hands.

"Well, it's pretty simple, Ezra. You pick up whatever you can carry in the street and toss it into one of the truck beds. Then you do that over and over again. We usually work from around nine to four with an hour break at noon. You get paid by the day. Funds show up in your account within twenty-four hours. That's the long and short of it. You got your phone? I'll scan your profile, and you're good to go."

I produce my phone, and Zeke hovers the tablet over it until they sync. He then taps a few buttons.

"You're all set," he says. "And Coop, make sure he doesn't keel over. It won't be good for morale."

"I'll do what I can."

As we walk towards the rubble, Coop says, "Don't mind him. He's a good guy. He just likes breaking balls. So, where should we start?"

"I'm just along for the ride."

Coop swings his pack to his chest. He removes two pairs of gloves and hands a set to me.

"I've got water in here. Make sure you drink it. Let's start over there," he says, pointing to a patch where no one else is.

He puts his gloves on, picks up a concrete slab, and heads off to the dump truck. I search the debris, pick out a manageable chunk and follow Coop. My body moves slowly, and I do half the amount Coop does in the first hour. I don't take anything too heavy, not wanting to risk my back flaring up. The work is monotonous; after two hours, sweat drenches my clothes, and the area seems like we barely made a dent. As I get into a rhythm—bend, lift, walk, toss, walk, bend, lift, walk, toss—my mind wanders. I try to remember what buildings used to stand here. Where did all the people go that used to live here? Are they dead? Did they leave? Are they happier wherever they went? My arms weaken after some time, and then all I can think about is putting one foot in front of the other. I'd hate to embarrass Coop by passing out. The relief must show on my face when he hands me a water bottle and tells me it's lunchtime.

"Looks like you could use a break," he says.

"What gave it away?" I say between breaths.

People are lining up at some food trucks parked across the street. I shuffle off in their direction, but Coop stops me.

"I brought some food for you if you want. It's not much, but it'll let you save some of your earnings from the day."

"You did?"

"Yeah."

Coop picks a stretch of sidewalk in the shade for us to sit down. He opens his pack and hands me an apple and another sandwich, peanut butter, and fluff, from the looks of it. I hold the food in my hands and somehow feel ashamed taking it.

"Don't you need this for your family?" I say.

"You are family."

"You know what I mean." I glance at the boots and the jeans and the shirt, and the food. "You don't have to do this, you know."

"What?" he says, taking a bite from the sandwich.

"Pity me."

He swallows and takes a swig of water.

"It's not like that."

"What's it like then?" I snap back.

Coop shakes his head, "If it were a problem for us or it was putting us out, I wouldn't do it. Ok? And I don't pity you. I feel for you. It's a big difference. So don't be an asshole."

His bluntness causes me to chuckle. It's twice now in two days that I've laughed. The more I do it, the less strange it's becoming.

"Glad to see some things haven't changed," I say.

He grins, "Some people just need to be told how it is."

I open the sandwich and take a bite. It's stale, but I eat the whole thing. Coop stretches his legs out. He bites into his apple, gazing at the work site.

"It's funny," he says. "Before all this, I always felt like I didn't have enough. Like I always needed more. Now that a lot of it is gone, I wonder why I ever wanted half of the stuff I was striving to get. I don't even miss most of the stuff I had. I wasted so much time chasing shit. Like I read a book the other week. I can't remember the last time I did that. It's weird. Did we just get to a point where we had too much? And it came to this to make us realize that? I don't know."

"We overcomplicated our lives."

"Yeah, exactly. No other species has what we have, and they don't seem any worse for wear. Animals, bugs, fish, they have nothing. We have everything, and yet we're miserable. How'd we get so far off track?"

"I didn't know you became a philosopher in your spare time."

He laughs, then falls quiet. When he finishes his apple, he tosses the core into a garbage can and pulls his gloves on. The trucks are returning with empty beds.

"Ready to get back to it?" he says, holding his hand out.

I grab it, and he hoists me to my feet. We saunter back to the pile we were working on, and the process starts over. An hour goes by, and I'm sore and tired, but I'm still going. We work until two-thirty, then take a short water break. I'll be hurting tomorrow; that much I know. I wipe the sweat from my face, ready for the final push of the day. The section I'm at is mostly large pieces that one of the tractors will have to lift. I find another spot that looks doable. I make one trip, then another. On the third, I remove a brick and freeze at what I've uncovered. It takes me a second to realize what it is since there's so much dust on it.

A hand. A child's hand.

I pry away more bricks, not bothering to bring them to the truck. I expose the arm. More bricks crash to the pavement, then I see the child's hair, and I slow down. The next chunk I can tell will let me see their face. All I can do is hold my breath and pull. The piece gives way, dropping at my feet. It's a boy, I think. I can't tell what race, as the layer of dust coating his face makes him look like a Roman marble statue. Judging by his size and the definition of his face, I put him at maybe five years old. A trail of dried blood lines his chin. His eyes are closed, and his mouth is locked open as if trapped in a scream. A piece of bone juts out near his collarbone.

My legs go numb then, and I fall to my knees. Any personal progress I made, I can feel unraveling. I think of Isla. I think of our unborn child. I think of this child and what the world has lost. I peel my gloves off and take the boy's hand, not knowing what else to do. His fingers are dry and cool, and rigid. I squeeze the tiny hand slightly, hoping he's just sleeping and will wake up any second. A muffled noise comes from behind me. I think someone is shouting my name, but I can't hear over the buzzing in my ears. Then there are hands all over me. Two take hold of an arm. One on my shoulder. Two under my armpits. I'm being lifted and pulled away from the boy. I let go of his hand. The fingers remain in place, outstretched as if reaching out for me to save him. Other people swarm into the area, and the boy vanishes from my sight. Whoever carries me sets me down on a knee-high piece of debris. The hands let me go. Coop stands in front of me, and he's saying something. I see his lips moving. I'm pretty sure he's speaking my name. I knew I wasn't ready for this. I should have never come here. Coop slaps me hard across the face, jolting me back into the moment.

"Ezra," he says. "Are you alright?"

I blink as the blood rushes back into my cheek. Something wet coats my face, and I can't tell if it's sweat or I've been crying. I nod towards the boy.

"Is he going to be ok?" I ask.

Coop looks at the people removing the debris, then back at me as if I just asked him if elephants could fly. He rubs his neck, not looking at me.

"He'll be taken care of," Coop says. "There's usually no more work for the day when we find...that type of thing. Let me grab my stuff. I'll walk you back to your place. Unless you want to eat over. I'm sure everyone would love to see you."

"No," I say, forcing myself unsteadily to my feet. "I'm fine. Don't worry about me. I just need some rest."

"I should've warned you about that possibility. I'm sorry, man, that's on me."

I give him a reassuring tap with my fist on his shoulder.

"Thanks for the sandwich and everything today," I say.

"I'll see you tomorrow?" he commands but tries to hide behind a question.

I nod but don't say the words, not wanting to give him false hope. An ambulance arrives, and I take that as my cue to leave. The faint sounds of crying hit me. The urge to turn back is overwhelming. I keep my shoulders forward and head home.

Blocks fade away. Images of the boy won't leave me alone. Did the end come quickly for him? Did he suffer? If he wasn't killed instantly, how long did he hold out hope that someone would rescue him? These are the thoughts I have now. The fact makes me sick to my stomach. It's a struggle to keep my sandwich down.

I get to my block and notice another bus in front of a building diagonal from mine. Maybe about twenty people are standing out front. A few kids are with their parents looking lost and scared. One of the people looks like the woman who settled me into my building. From her body language, she's arguing with a group of four adults. A guy is standing off to the side of the group, smoking a cigarette. He squints at me as I approach.

"You supposed to live here too?" he asks me. The guy is wearing a green sweatshirt, khaki shorts, and colorful flip-flops. His skin is a weathered tan that makes him appear older than he probably is.

"No," I say. "I'm across the street. What's going on?"

"Someone thinks they found a bomb in there. No one wants to go in, but we've nowhere else to go."

"A bomb?"

"Yeah, I guess that's been the case with a lot of these buildings over here that the Right used to occupy. Before they fled the city, they booby trapped the hell out of any buildings they could get into as a last fuck you to the Left. This one here is brand new, from what I hear. No one has ever lived in it yet."

"Really."

The guy nods as he inhales on his cigarette. "Only a block over. The same thing killed five people in the last week. The military has cleared out, so getting someone to disarm the things is next to impossible. These buildings were supposed to be the spoils of war. Give everyone that got displaced during the fighting the empty homes that aren't being used anymore. Surprise, surprise, it's not working out as they wanted."

The main woman is on her phone now. An unease bristles amongst the group. I nod goodbye to the smoker and cross the street. On the first floor of my building, the rattle of pots and pans comes down the hall as dinner preparations begin. I take the elevator to the fifth floor and enter the solitude of my studio apartment. The setting sun casts the living room in a warm glow. I drop into the loveseat to catch my breath. In the quiet, with nothing to do, it doesn't take long for my mind to wander into the dark voids. The boy's stiff fingers reaching for me come to the forefront of my thoughts. Then to Isla. The visuals, the memories, cause me to cry. When I can't take any more of it, I stagger out to the balcony. I move to the rail. One leap, and it can all be over. A blip of pain, and then I'd hurt no longer. The temptation beckons me like Homer's sirens. My fingers curl around the railing. I want this to end, but something keeps me in place. The finality of the decision gives me pause.

As I'm building the courage to hurl myself over the edge, shouting from the street distracts me. I find where the shouts are coming from and see the people outside the rigged building. Booby traps. Those bastards. I wonder what they could've rigged up. How complex could the setups be? If some are wired or have electrical components, I imagine that wouldn't be too challenging to disarm. Stop. Focus. I need to focus on what I'm doing. Over the side. Stop the pain. That's my goal right now. But what if I get it wrong, trying to disarm the explosives? Meet the same fate, wouldn't I? And at least that way, my death would have a little more glory. I debate my options for another minute, then retreat into the apartment. I grab my Leatherman, and I'm out the door before I can change my mind.

Chapter 6

I stomp across the street and push my way through the group of people. The lead woman is sitting on the steps to the building with a phone to her ear. She's dressed in white cigarette pants, midnight blue flats, and a denim button-down. Her hair reminds me of a coconut husk in both its color and wild strands. A sour look comes over her when she realizes I'm coming up to her. She puts the phone to her chest as she talks to me.

"Listen, I don't have an update for you yet," she says.

"Where's the explosive?" I ask.

She rises from the steps coming eye level with me. Her lips roll together as she sizes me up.

"What did you say?"

"Where's the explosive?"

She hesitates, then puts the phone to her ear, "I'm going

to have to call you back."

The phone stays in her hand as she lowers it to her side. Suspicion swirls in her eyes.

"Who're you?"

"Ezra," I say.

"Just a concerned citizen," she says with an attitude.

"More than welcome to deal with it yourself."

She sighs, "Sorry, it's just been a long few weeks. A rep told me this place was swept and was move-in ready, but apparently, that was a load of crap. What am I supposed to tell these people now? You know that place to stay we promised you? Oh, sorry, no can do. I hear sleeping on the street is comfortable. We're no better than the other side if we don't deliver on what we say." She catches herself rambling. "You know what, sorry, that's not relevant right now. You really want to go in there?"

"I can take a look?"

"Your funeral," she says, then turns and gives me a wave to follow her.

We move past the entrance. The space is dim, lit by a single bulb. Straight ahead, there are two doors on the left wall. Directly to my right is another door. To the left of this door is a stairwell attached to the wall. She points towards the stairs.

"Tripwire is on the second step," she says.

"Move everyone back across the street. Don't send anyone in here until I come out."

"You're serious about this?"

"Are you trying to talk me out of it?"

She shrugs, "If you're sure." Her hand is on the door, about to leave, when she turns back. "I'm Evelyn, by the way."

I don't say anything, so she leaves. I wait a few minutes, not moving, letting the air settle and allowing my ears to adjust to the sounds of the hallway. Using my phone light, I scan every inch of the floors and the walls, trying to spot anything that seems out of place. Then I focus on the floor, letting the phone light my path. Baby steps. Don't rush anything. With each foot that goes down, I test the pressure for any give before committing all of my weight. I repeat this until I get to the stairs. I ease into a crouch to inspect the situation. My eyes run over the stairs with the motion of an old typewriter.

On the second step, I spot the wire. It's thin but visible. Maybe a violin string. I trace it to where the stairs meet the wall. The wire loops around the head of a screw half sunk into the wall. Reversing course, I follow the wire to the banister. Something protrudes from behind one of the spires, but I can't quite tell what it is from my vantage point. I flash my phone to my left, checking for any other obstructions. Nothing. Staying crouched, I pivot to the side of the stairwell. The light shines on the object. My mind flashes through every action movie I've ever watched, and I'm pretty sure I'm staring at a hand grenade. It looks like it's held in place by about half a roll of clear packing tape. I bend in close and see the wire attached to the grenade's pin.

The pressure of a foot pulling the wire would rip the pin from the grenade, setting it off. The rationale seems sound to me. So all I should have to do is sever the wire, and as long as the pin doesn't come out, I shouldn't be blown to pieces. As I maneuver back to the step, I realize I've been holding my breath. I release it slowly and take out my Leatherman. Unfolding it, I reconfigure it so the pliers with the wire cutter are the primary tool. The sound of my heart is all I can hear as I bend in close. I open the pliers and center the wire between the cutter. My eyes lock onto the pin of the grenade. In a few seconds, I'll be either pumped full of shrapnel or right where I left off. My hand squeezes. The pliers close. Click. Two ends of the wire fall to the step. I don't move, counting the beats in my head. One. Two. Three. Four...Twenty comes, and I consider myself safe.

I close the pliers and unfold the knife. With my left hand, I secure the grenade in place. The roundness of it dips down as it meets the flat part of the spire, creating a pocket of space. I insert the blade here and apply the lightest force for it to cut through the tape. Once I'm through, I peel the grenade back and cut through the other side of the tape. I remove a strip of adhesive left over on the spire and wrap it around the grenade, securing the clasp from any accidents. The hallway returns to life, and the outside sounds are again present. Sweat coats my forehead. As the adrenaline eases off, something hits me—a realization. I'm still alive.

I stuff the grenade in my pocket and head outside. It takes me a minute to find Evelyn. When I do, I wave her over. She hurries across the street.

"Well?" she says.

"I removed it."

"Seriously?"

I reach into my pocket and pull the grenade halfway out for her to see. Her face pales at the sight of it.

"Wow. Ok. Geez," Evelyn says, taking a step back from me.

I hide the grenade and ask, "How many apartments are in the building?"

"What?"

"Looks like three floors. How many rooms?"

"Uh," she says, staring at my pocket. Then she focuses on my face. "There's three per floor. So nine total."

"Can you get me into every room?"

She squints at me suspiciously. "Yeah, why?"

"They could've left more," I say. "I can check each apartment. Make sure they're clear before you let everyone in."

Evelyn lets out a short, sweet laugh.

"What's your story, buddy?" she says in disbelief.

I shrug and say, "No story."

"Yeah, right. With guys like you, there's always a story."

"'Guys like me'?"

She smoothes a patch of wild hair back, gazing into my eyes as if they'll give her the answers she wants. When they provide her with nothing, she asks, "How long do you think it'd take?"

"I'm not sure."

Her attention turns to the group of people huddled together. The drop-off bus has left, leaving her with few options. She doesn't want to disappoint them but doesn't like the idea of a total stranger's death on her hands. I get that, so I try to help her by placing my hand on her phone.

"I took your phone, if anyone asks," I tell her. "This is my choice, not yours. Whatever happens, it's my decision."

"I can't ask you to do that."

"You're not asking. Just let go. It's as easy as that."

Her fingers are still clenched around the phone as she searches my face.

"Whatever happens to me... I'm prepared for," I say. "That's my story."

Shaking her head, she pulls her hand with the phone back from me. Her fingers fly over the screen, and then she holds the bottom end toward me.

"Scan your imprint, and you'll be an authorized user."

I obey her command. Then she taps a few more things and

hands the phone over.

"Ezra, was it?" she says.

"That's right."

She smiles and whispers, "Thank you."

Something about the way she says the words makes me feel lighter. I shove the emotion aside and disappear into the building of hidden dangers.

The door next to the stairs is the first room I pick. With a wave of the phone over the imprint scanner, the door unlocks. I don't immediately open the door. Everything needs to be slow and deliberate. Rushing is the surest way for me to meet my maker. I grip the handle, twist the knob, and pry the door open an inch at a time. Once I can see a crack of light on the other side of the door, I fire up my phone light again and give the edges of the door a quick once over. My breath cuts out as I see the glint of wire sagging across where a chain lock would typically be. Careful not to disturb anything, I close the door and lock the Leatherman into the previous configuration. There's no way to know for sure, but I'm hoping whoever rigged this place used the same setup inside. I crack the door again and snip the wire. Click. I pause. After I finish counting, I ease the door open just far enough for me to slip inside the room. Mounted to the wall is another grenade. I cut it down and drop it into my pocket.

Darkness floods the apartment, so my first instinct is to flip the light switch, but I stop myself. Could something be wired into the lights? I don't know if that's a thing or how advanced these traps are. I err on the side of caution and just use my phone. From where I'm standing, I'm in the main living area. The layout looks similar to where I'm staying—compact design to maximize the space. Minimal furniture decorates the room.

Probably the staging furniture, if I had to guess. It should make this job easier with fewer places to hide things.

I sweep the light over the floor before I move. My feet follow the trail I set with the beam. The system is effective for moving around. I pick the kitchen first and go through each cabinet, drawer, and appliance. Nothing. In the living room, I check each cushion on the couch and chair and again find nothing. There are two bedrooms. In the master, I locate and disarm one more grenade attached to the sliding doors of a closet. My vigilance remains high throughout the search of the rest of the apartment. I don't turn up any more.

Creeping into the living room, I sit on the couch and think about the placement of the grenades. The stairs make sense. It's a natural movement in an easily accessible place to rig the explosive. Same with the doors. Unless you knew to look for them, most people would barge right in. They wouldn't even know what happened—gone instantly, unaware of how or why. The use of tape to mount them and the quantity in the apartment make me think they didn't want to take too much time, which makes sense, I guess. The spite that went into the strategy heats my blood. More confident, I reach the light switch, hesitating a second before flipping it. A single bulb illuminates the room. I retrace my steps through the apartment, turning the lights on and double-checking that I left no stone unturned. In a pantry closet, I notice an abandoned tote bag. I grab it and head to the living room, where I load the wrapped grenades into the bag. At the door, I take one last look, feeling good that the apartment is safe, then I step into the hallway.

The process is the same for the remaining two rooms on the first floor. Mostly, there isn't any variation in the location of the grenades. Both entryways carry the small explosives, as do the closets. The third apartment has one extra hidden in the shower. My phone tells me it's close to six o'clock. That means the first floor took me over two hours to clear. In the third apartment, I turn on the faucet in the kitchen sink and wash my face, then tilt my head to quench my thirst. Using the sleeve of my shirt, I dry off. With the deadliest bag of groceries in tow, I ascend to the second floor. An initial analysis of the second flight of steps doesn't reveal any trip wires, so I head into the first room by the stairs. The door lacks any rigging, and I don't find any grenades in the apartment. Apartments two and three turn up empty as well. Maybe whoever's idea it was to booby trap the place stuck to the first floor, figuring that the damage inflicted on the first wave would deter others. It seems plausible, but I climb to the third floor, assuming I'm wrong.

After the stairs and the first apartment turn up without grenades, I move faster through the last two apartments. Fifteen minutes before ten, I deem the entire building safe. I clamber down the three flights and emerge into the cool nighttime air. To my surprise, the people are sitting huddled across the street. I expected them to have left. I have no idea where they would've gone, but I didn't think they'd still be here. As I approach, some of them stir.

"Is Evelyn here?" I ask no one in particular.

Her voice rings out to my left. "Hey, I'm here." She pushes through the group, stopping close to me. "Still standing," she grins.

"Still standing," I say, holding her phone for her to take. "Every room should be good."

As she takes her phone, she nods at the tote bag.

"Do a little shopping while you were in there?"

"Not sure how good of a diet it'd be."

She laughs with a soft, gentle easiness that strikes a chord in my heart. People in the group are on their feet, nudging others awake. Evelyn faces them and says, "Good news, everyone. Ezra here removed all of the explosives in the building. I can get you moved in now."

The group is worn and slow-moving, but one of them claps. After a few rounds, others join in until it seems they're all clapping. I almost start doing it too, when I realize they're clapping for me. As if I did something worthy of praise. If I had died, I wouldn't have thought twice about it. I wouldn't have thought about anything ever again. They don't know that, though. The clapping fades away, and they shuffle toward their new home. Some of them pat me on the back as they leave.

"Can I get you some food or something?" Evelyn says. "I feel that's the least I could do."

I hold the tote up and say, "I really should figure out what to do with these."

"Well, try not to blow yourself up."

She smiles, turns, stops, and comes back. "Hey, would you be willing to do something like this again? I think I could work the system so you could get paid for it. I'm responsible for these moves regularly. It would be great to avoid this happening again."

"I don't know," I mumble. "I'll think about it."

"Ok. Can I give you my number in case you're interested?"

I nod and hold out my phone. Evelyn taps on hers, then passes it over mine, transferring her details.

"Have a good night, Ezra," she smiles. "And thank you."

I watch her on the sidewalk until she disappears into the building. Once she's gone, I glance at the tote and consider my disposal options. The police are an option, but I honestly don't know if they're even a thing at this point. Would they arrest me for showing up at the station with a bag of explosives? Looking the way I do right now, I don't think they'd buy my story. I can't just leave them for someone to find. If I toss them in the trash, I could risk hurting whoever empties the Dumpsters. I could bury them, but where and with what tools? Then I remember the river. When the construction of D.C. Two began, the government also built a bridge across one of the inlets. If that's still intact, I can drop them into the river. No one swims out there and it should be deep enough that it wouldn't interfere with any boats passing over them.

With nothing else to do, I head for the bridge. Half a mile over, the city is in shambles. I wonder how bad the other sections are. It feels worse than the news let on. This area is shrouded in a darkness that I'm not used to. It dawns on me that there's no electricity here. Any lights I see in the few structures still standing are weak and sway with the movement of candles. The streets aren't passable for cars, creating a silence like I'm walking through a museum. A few fires burn in trash cans. The flames illuminate the faces of those hunched around them. Vacant eyes gaze into the fires, struggling to comprehend how this could've happened, how their lives got upended so easily. And there's disillusionment in those eyes. Eyes that have witnessed how fragile the system we'd built everything around truly was.

I've got a mile to go and my body is screaming for me to stop. A small reserve of energy stored somewhere deep inside is the only thing pushing me forward. The scent of the water lets me know I'm close. The outline of the bridge comes into view as I traverse a strip of rubble. It's hard to tell against the darkness, but it looks like there's damage a quarter of the way up the bridge. I stumble around until I locate the entrance to the pedestrian walkway. After ten minutes of scuffling through the blackness, my foot suddenly drops out from beneath me. I topple forward as my legs plummet through a gaping hole blown out of the path big enough to swallow me. My heart rate spikes as my free hand lashes out for anything to hold. I get a solid grip on the edge of busted cement. Over my shoulder, I can make out the glint of the water flowing past. It would be at least a fifty-foot fall. All I have to do is let go, and gravity will take care of the rest. If the impact didn't do the job, drowning or hypothermia would finish things.

For some reason, my fingers stay locked in place. The part of me that I thought was gone isn't ready to give up. I never liked the water anyway. Slowly, I ease the tote of grenades to my chest, then slide it to my side. I push my arm as far from my body as I can and release the bag. A few seconds later, I hear the confirmation splash. With my other hand free, I place it against the opposite wall for a second point of contact. In unison, I push and pull until I'm far enough onto the ground that I can shimmy my legs out. The events of the day have finally caught up to me. My tank's run dry. Just the thought of walking back to the apartment makes me more exhausted. I rest against the cement before I push to my feet. The hole is apparent now, and I'm careful to climb around it. Stumbling out of the walkway, I spot a bench overlooking the river on a stretch of grass. It beckons to me, and I answer its call. I lie down, and I'm asleep in seconds.

WEEK 10 - NOVEMBER 23

The caw of seagulls wakes me—nine forty-five, my phone reads. I move to a seated position, rubbing the sleep from my eyes.

My joints are stiff and a bit cold, so I set a course for the apartment to get the blood flowing. For the first time in weeks, I feel hungry. I walk west for a while, hoping to hit a patch of the city not destroyed. Some cars start passing me, and the hustle and bustle of life grows louder. I cut north, following the sound until I find what I'm looking for. It's a familiar section of the city known for its restaurants, and I'm glad to see it doesn't look like it sustained much bomb damage. A stark contrast to everywhere else I've been so far. Many first-floor stores shuttered their doors, but a few remain open. I duck into one that has a neon sign spelling out the word coffee.

The place smells of flour and fresh bread. It's warm in the small interior, which I welcome. An older man with a bald head and white mustache inspects me over the glass counter containing an assortment of baked goods. His demeanor isn't inviting. I make a mental note to shave as soon as possible.

"You need something?" the man says. He has a slight accent, but I can't tell from where.

"I could use a cup of coffee and a bagel if you've got it."

"Do you have money?"

"What's that going to cost?"

The man squints at me as if he's making up a cost based solely on my appearance.

"Twenty," he says.

"Seems a little high."

"Times are tough. Ingredients are hard to come by. You want to pay or not?"

I check my digital wallet on my phone. The meager funds came through from my day's work of moving debris. The two items will take a sizable chunk out of the earnings. But what use do I have for money now?

"I'll pay. Coffee black. Everything bagel if you've got it. Cream cheese if you've got that too."

"Cream cheese is another five."

"Another five?"

He shrugs, "That's business."

I scan my phone at the register. The man continues to inspect me with an air of disgust. When the payment goes through, he goes to a back counter, fills a cup with coffee, puts a lid on, and hands it to me.

"Bagel toasted?" he asks.

I nod. He extracts a large bagel from the glass counter. He slices it, then toasts it and applies the cream cheese. Once done, he wraps it in paper and drops it on the countertop.

I swipe it and grumble a thanks; then, I'm back on the street. I polish off the bagel in record time and sip the coffee as I go. It doesn't take long before I'm back in the ruins. From the looks of it, people are still trying to make a go of living in the buildings despite the battering they took. Sheets drape across sections where walls used to stand. Wires snake out from doorways and windows, leading to an entanglement along a power hub. They must be overloading the systems big time. It's not a wonder there are so many rolling blackouts and a lack of stable electricity. I'd be drowning in overtime for months if I still had my old job. Kids roam the streets, many looking just as worn out as I do. School, I'm guessing, is shut down. If they still have parents, they must be going out of their minds. Other people I come across are busying themselves with clearing a path through the rubble to get into their old homes. Another pair are drilling and hammering in a new door frame.

I walk north until I hit the street leading straight to my apartment. It takes me another hour to get back. As I'm about to get to the door of the building, an older black guy and a boy—freshly turned a teenager—approach me. It looks like they've been waiting.

"Are you Ezra?" the older guy says.

"Yes," I reply.

"Name's Benson. This is my grandson, Davis."

The man is as tall as I am, lean, with a handsome face and sharp eyes. He's supporting himself on a cane, giving him a hunched appearance. His clothes have the tint of gray from that dust that seems to attach itself to every surface. One of his shoes lacks laces and stretches wide. I guess he's got a foot wound. The teenager is medium height and skinny with similar looks as his grandfather. He's a step back as if he's hiding.

"Do I know you?" I ask.

"Nope," Benson says. "But there were some rumblings last night. We know Evelyn. She told us what you did. Told us where to find you."

"Did she?"

Benson points at the building across the street with his cane. "She told us you cleared out the entire building by yourself."

I shrug, "I might have."

"Any chance we can enlist your services? We're only two blocks over."

"My services?"

"That's right," he says. Sensing some hesitation from me, he then quickly adds. "We don't have a lot in the way of money, but we can trade you something for your time."

"It's not that," I say, scratching my beard. "I'm surprised you heard about that already."

"Somebody that gives a damn and is willing to help. That's a rare commodity these days. Word of that spreads real quick."

"Have you been in there? Have you seen the mines?"

"Davis thinks he saw one."

"That right?" I ask Davis.

He nods but doesn't say anything.

"Tell him where you saw it," Benson prompts him.

"In the stairwell on the second floor."

"How'd you know it was a mine?" I ask.

"They showed photos of them on TV."

"What'd it look like?"

Davis holds his hands a foot apart. "It was about this long. Round and kind of sloped. Some gooey stuff was coming out of one end with some wires."

Sounds a bit more advanced than the grenades.

"What do you think?" Benson says.

I pause a moment, then say, "Give me ten minutes. I'll see what I can do."

Benson winces from the pain of shifting the cane to his opposite hand so he can shake mine.

"Appreciate it," he says.

In the apartment, I wash my face with cold water, then change into the second set of clothes Coop gave me. When I return to the street, I see Benson and Davis seated on a stoop of the adjacent building. Davis helps Benson to his feet, and we're off. They stop outside a four-story building riddled with bullet holes and splotches of charred brick from street-level RPGs. The fourth floor looks like it suffered a strike, but the remainder is intact, aside from a few smashed windows.

"This is the place," Benson says.

"It's big," I say, sizing the place up. "This will take me a while."

"We'll make do."

"There power here?"

"It comes and goes."

"If you can scrounge me up a proper flashlight, it'll help."

Benson flicks his head at Davis. Davis nods in silent understanding, then takes off.

"He's good at scavenging," Benson says. "He should be able to find one."

"Everything unlocked?"

"Most of the apartments were set up with cameras during the fighting. The news said it was a smart thing to do. It looks like it was decent advice. If a door's locked, whoever lives there knows their place is safe. If it's unlocked, and you find it in your heart to check it out, great. Otherwise, it's more the stairwells we were hoping you could investigate for us."

"Alright," I say and start towards the entrance.

"Hey," Benson stops me. "In case things go...well...in case you don't come out. Is there anyone you want me to notify?"

I shake my head and say, "It's just me." Benson bobs his head and avoids eye contact. I keep walking. Once inside, I stop and get my bearings. Two doors are on each of the side walls. On the back wall is an elevator in the center with a door to the stairwell on the left. Benson is concerned with the stairwell, so I start there. Phone light in hand, I take the same slow, methodical approach, cracking the door ajar and scanning for any wires. When I don't see any, I enter. A layer of dust, glass, and debris coats the steps. This job isn't going to be the same as the other, I can tell already. Expectations, I should've set some for Benson. He may be disappointed with what I can do. Davis said the device he saw was on the second floor.

In the debris, I root out a metal rod. As I creep through the space, I use the rod to move aside loose objects or to lightly probe beneath the dust for any connection with something hidden. Finding nothing, I move to the stairs. Step by step, I sweep the light over the surface, studying every detail. At the second-floor landing, nestled in the corner, I spot the mine. It's exactly how Davis described it. Out of the top end is a thick white substance. Jutting out of it is a pencil-shaped-looking stick. Attached are wires that loop down to a square that holds two double A batteries. Stemming from that is another small-looking device. Electrical tape wraps the wires at two points. Other than that, I don't see anything else. If there are batteries and wires, then something electrical is going on. It's overall a simple-looking device, which is good as it limits my options of how it can work. The white stuff, I assume, is explosive. Based on the batteries, the stick may deliver an electrical charge that sets off something inside the explosives.

I don't know if movement has anything to do with how it can be triggered. Every move I make, I keep that in mind. Sweat is forming on my palms, so I use some dust from the ground to soak it up. I plan to remove the power source, then the wires, and if I haven't been blown to a million pieces, I'll try to pick up the mine. The sound of my heart radiates into my ears. I prop my phone up next to the mine. My Leatherman comes out next. If I survive this, I have to do some research on explosives.

I get the pliers out on the multitool and then set them next to my phone. The tape is where I start. With the nail of my thumb, I peel back a corner. As slow and steady as I can, I unwrap the tape. Once it's off, I move to the second piece. Perspiration beads on my forehead. I aim for any drops I feel slipping off my skin to land in empty patches of ground. I don't want anything disturbing the mine and have it go off. The distance I am to the mine would incinerate the entirety of my face.

I push the thoughts aside and grab the Leatherman. Holding my breath, I snip the wires on both ends of the battery pack to ensure no power travels through them. I do the same for the other electronic device attached. So far, so good. I sit back for a moment, massaging my hands and wiping the dampness from my face. When my heart rate slows, I pinch the stick-like object in the goo and slide it out. Everything is disassembled, which gives me confidence that it won't go off if I pick the mine up. I grab my phone, then tilt the mine a few inches, checking to see if anything else is attached. Nothing. Perfect. I cradle the mine in my hands. One down. One life saved.

I place the mine out of the way, then head outside. Benson sits across the street at a rusty white wire folding table. On the table is a chess board. Davis contemplates a move across from Benson. When Davis sees me, he hops out of the matching white wire chair and picks up a plastic bag.

"I got you what you asked for," Davis says. He opens the bag and fishes out a medium-sized black Maglite. "I found this too, which I thought would be useful." The next thing he brings out is a helmet light. He hands them both to me. I depress each button, and they click to life with solid and powerful beams.

"Good work," I say.

Davis grins with a sense of pride.

"How's it going in there?" Benson asks.

"I found the one that was on the second-floor stairwell. I got it disarmed. I'm going to need something else."

"Name it," Benson says.

"Can you find me a roll of that bubble wrapping stuff? You know the clear sheets in shipping packages that you can pop. And then I'd need a large bag, preferably a backpack that I can stuff these things in."

"You heard the man," Benson says to Davis.

Davis doesn't waste any time. He sprints off on his next mission.

"Looks like you could use a drink," Benson says. He motions for me to sit down in Davis' chair. From a little cooler under the table, Benson produces a bottle of water. I drink half the bottle, then dump the other half over my head. It's ice cold and feels incredible on my hot skin.

"His parents got killed the first day the fighting broke out," Benson says. He's studying the chess board as he talks. "He came to live with me after. We held out for as long as we could, but the fighting got too intense. I took a stray bullet to my foot. We didn't have much choice once that happened. Barely made it to a Safety Zone. The doctors did what they could for my foot, but it still hasn't fully healed. When the government told us we could come home, I didn't know this was what I would be coming back to. One of Davis' friends got killed by a mine a week ago. He doesn't talk much now. You should feel honored he spoke to you."

Benson picks up a pawn absentmindedly, rolling it around in his fingers.

"We've been bouncing around from place to place. It's no way for a kid to be raised. Politicians make all these promises, but when the time comes for them to follow through, they always disappoint you. Last few days, we've been sleeping in a parking garage."

He returns the pawn to its square; then, he removes a hand-kerchief from his pocket and dabs at the corner of his eyes. We're quiet for a bit. When all the distractions are gone, it's easy to get lost in contemplation. Benson clears his throat and sits forward.

"You get scared messing with those bombs?" he asks.

I shrug. "Sometimes. I don't know. It's complicated. Most days, I don't feel anything at all. On other days I feel too much. You know?"

Benson grunts.

"I think about the kids, and fear doesn't come into it," I say. "If someone's got to go, I'd rather it be me than them." Having admitted that out loud to another person makes me feel self-conscious. I don't know this man, but for some reason, I don't want him to judge me. To think less of me for what I said. Before Benson can comment, I stand and say, "I should get back to it. If he gets the bubble wrap, give me a shout."

Benson studies me for a moment, then says, "Ok."

I take the two lights and head to the stairwell. The Maglite I tuck inside my pants along my hip. The headlight is uncomfortable but makes it easier to have my hands free. I move to the third floor but don't see any mines. On the fourth floor, I find one with the same setup. Using the same process as the first mine, I disarm it in minutes. Now that the stairwell is clear, I try the doors. The fourth floor is locked up solid. Same with the third. On the second floor, two knobs turn, unlocked. Most of the furniture is missing in these apartments. Personal belongings lie scattered around as if the vibrations from the bombs and RPGs shook them from their shelves. These apartments are more significant than the ones from last night too. The dust seeping in from shattered windows and the junk lying around make the sweep a time-consuming ordeal. Each apartment takes me over an hour and results in one more mine. I clear the second floor and then try the doors on the first floor. None are open. I make my way back through the stairwell to the fourth floor and gather up the mines, stacking them by the building entrance.

Benson slouches in his chair, sleeping. Davis is sitting on the curb, picking aimlessly at his shoe. Another bag is by his side.

"How'd you luck out?" I ask him.

He flinches at my voice, then recognizes me. "Is this what you needed?" He says, handing me the bag. Inside is a thick roll of bubble wrap. Davis stands and gives me a backpack that he's sitting on.

"This is perfect," I say. "How'd you get all this stuff?"

He shrugs and grins but doesn't give me an answer.

"Well, you're a legend in my book, kid," I say and hold my hand out for him to shake. He hesitates, then takes hold of my hand. "I'm going to wrap the mines up and be on my way. Tell your grandfather you should be all set. If you see any more, you know where to find me."

"Ok," Davis says.

In the hallway, I unspool the bubble wrap on the floor. I place one mine down at the edge and roll it up until a substantial cushion forms. Will this make any difference in them accidentally going off while I transport them? Who knows, but it puts my mind at ease. I stuff each into the backpack lengthwise. The zippers won't close; however, they're packed so tightly that they shouldn't move while I'm walking. I sit on the floor, loop my arms through the straps, then roll to all fours and push to a standing position. The mines are heavier than I hoped. It's going to be a long walk to the bridge.

Outside, Davis runs up and hands me another bottle of water.

"Thanks," I say. "I'll see you around."

Twenty minutes into my trek, I drain three-quarters of

the water bottle and dump the rest on my head. It does little to cool me off. A memory of Isla comes to me then. We went hiking one weekend in hopes of seeing a sunset. Towards the mountain peak we were on, she slipped and twisted her ankle. I carried her down the whole way on my back like my dad used to do when I was a kid. The weight of the mines reminds me of her, and I think she's there again for a moment.

"I think we need to stop ordering so much Chinese food," I mumble to myself. That was the crack I made to Isla at the time, which resulted in her pinching my neck so hard I thought a bee stung me. "I almost dropped you," I mumble again, reliving the day. A gust of wind carries the water droplets across my neck. It feels like her lips kissing the spot where she'd pinched me. "I miss you," I say, but no one answers. A bus drives by, and the noise makes me alert again. I suddenly feel embarrassed for talking to myself and continue the remainder of the walk in silence.

It's past five o'clock, so I can see the bridge now. No vehicles are on it, so I elect to walk on the road instead of the walkway that almost sent me to a watery grave. Near the middle of the bridge, I drop the backpack and take out a mine. I unwrap it and heave it over the rail, watching until it splashes into the water. When the pack is empty, I roll the bubble wrap into a single roll and stuff it in the bag. The breeze is cool here, so I rest my arms over the rail and gaze at the setting sun, having made it through another day.

Chapter 7

In the morning, I call Coop. There's a sense of alarm in his voice when he answers.

"Christ, Ezra," he says. "I thought you were...I thought maybe...I don't know what I thought. I came by yesterday morning, and you weren't there. I wasn't sure if something happened."

"I'm alright. And sorry. I got tied up in something else, which is why I'm calling."

"What's up?"

"Do you remember that guy we used to work with, Gary... Gary Ranger? He was one of the old timers."

"Yeah, what about him?"

"Do you have his number?"

"I think so. I'd have to check, though. Why do you want to talk to him?"

"He was in the Marines before he worked for Deakins, wasn't he?"

"Sounds familiar. Again, though, why?"

"Something I'm working on. I just had a few questions for him."

"What the hell are you working on that he could help you with that I couldn't? Come on, man, what's going on?"

I pause, take a deep breath, and then say, "I helped disarm some mines left in buildings. That's where I was the last two days."

A long silence answers me, then I hear Coop chuckle and say, "Ok. Good one. I'm glad you've got your sense of humor back."

"I'm serious."

"You're serious? What do you know about disarming mines?"

"I managed the ones I came across. They were pretty straightforward. But that's why I want to talk to Gary, see if he can give me some pointers."

Coop's quiet again. When he talks next, his voice turns serious.

"Listen, I know things haven't been easy, but...."

"Don't," I cut him off. "I don't need a lecture. All I need is his number. Do you have it or not?"

"Geez, ok. You don't have to get snippy. Give me a second."

Coop drops off, then is back on a minute later.

"Alright, I just texted you his contact information," he says.

"Thanks," I say, ready to hang up.

"Hey."

"Yeah."

"Be careful," Coop says.

"I will," I respond with less edge in my voice. "Thanks, Coop."

"Don't be a stranger."

"I won't."

I end the call, feeling a little bad for being short with Coop, but I know he'll get over it. The momentum I have with whatever this is, I want to keep rolling. If I stop now, I won't be any good to anyone. I tap Gary's number from my text messages. The phone rings. It rings for a while. I'm ready to hang up when a gruff voice answers.

"Hello?"

"Is this Gary?"

"Who wants to know?"

"My name is Ezra Asher. I worked for Jim Deakins' company, Helios Solar. I was on one of the repair crews."

"Asher, you said?"

"That's right."

"What can I do for you?"

"This might sound like an odd request, but I've been helping some people clear mines out of their homes. I know you served and saw the front lines. I was wondering if you might have any, I don't know, pointers for dealing with disarming them."

"Jesus, what're you doing that for? Deakins give you the boot or something?"

"No," I sigh. "Deakins was killed, or so I'm told, during the fighting. The agent I talked to said he was under investigation for possible dealings with the Right. So there's no company to go back to."

"Damn. I hadn't heard. When I left the company, I moved farther north. It sounds like you guys took a real beating there. The whole country's a mess. Only a matter of time before the same thing happens here."

I say, "Seeming that way."

"Well, to answer your question, I don't know much about

explosives, at least for what you're trying to do. I saw plenty of how fucking horrible IEDs are and what they do to people, but I wasn't responsible for disarming them."

"You weren't, huh? Well, it was worth a shot."

"Hang on," he says. "I got some buddies you can talk to. I'll give you Silas' number. He was one of the craziest bastards I've ever met. That guy wouldn't break a sweat even if he were dismantling an atomic bomb. He can probably help you out. I think he's not too far from you. He's a bit eccentric, just as a fair warning."

"I appreciate that."

"I'll send his info along. Good luck to ya."

I hang up, the new number buzzes through text, and I call Silas. Someone answers, but they don't say anything.

"Hello?" I say.

"How did you get this number?"

"Is this Silas?"

No response.

"Uh, Gary Ranger gave me your number. He said he served with you. My name is Ezra Asher. He gave me your name and said you might be able to help with some information about disarming IEDs."

No response.

"I'm sorry. Are you there?"

I hear the flick of a lighter and a deep inhale. Then he speaks.

"Gary's a good man. I don't like to talk on the phone, though. Never know who's listening."

"Oh, Ok. Gary said you might be somewhat local. Would you be willing to meet then?

Another long pause. Silas clears his throat and says, "Give me three hours. Don't leave." Then the line goes dead. I look at my phone, confirming the call is over. This should be interesting. I'm not sure how he will find me, but I guess I'll see in three hours.

To kill time, I grab my dirty clothes and wash them in the shower. On the balcony, I flip a stool from the kitchen and hang the clothes over the legs to dry. I can tell from cleaning the clothes that there's no hot water, but I need a cleaning. I let the water run for a while, preparing myself for the shock that's sure to come. The water hits my skin like a million ice cubes fired from a machine gun. It knocks the air right out of me. I scrub each area as fast as my hands will go, then turn the knob and hop out. As uncomfortable as the shower was, it gave me a boost of much-needed alertness. I towel off and get dressed in the last outfit from Coop.

Two hours to go. Sitting on the loveseat, I crave coffee and realize there are some essentials I could use. The cash balance on my phone isn't much, but I should be able to get some basics. I remember seeing a Dollar Tree a few blocks over that I'm pretty sure was still standing and open. Silas told me not to leave, but two hours should be enough time for me to make a quick trip. On a leftover napkin from the breakfast with Coop, I write a note, telling Silas I'll be back soon, in the offhand chance he beats me back here. I hold the napkin while I close the door, locking the note in place.

When I get to the Dollar Tree and walk in, the sight of the interior causes me to pause. The place looks like looters ransacked it. Lights dangle from the ceiling haphazardly. Shelves are bare, and products and torn boxes litter the floor. I'm about to leave when someone calls out to me.

"It's ok. We're open."

I lean further until I see a girl behind the counter. She

waves at me with a smile.

"Sorry, it's a bit of a mess. Today was a dropoff day, so people were a bit wild."

"Gotcha," I say, committing myself to the store. The shelves are picked over, but I scrounge together a three-pack of generic brand soap, single-ply toilet paper, a toothbrush, and toothpaste. I spot a razor, but it's too much money. Man, I could use a shave. Right now, though, I need to prioritize. There's one bag of coffee that I'm lucky to find. I scrape together a couple of cans of baked beans and some ramen for food. The girl rings me up, and I'm over what I've got left for money. I ditch the baked beans and the toothbrush.

"They're handing out meal replacement powder packs at some of the Safety Zones," the girl says. "They taste like crap, but they're free, and they'll keep you going. At least they've got some vitamins and stuff in them."

"Thanks for the tip."

"Sure thing," she says as she finishes tossing the groceries into a brown paper bag.

Back at the apartment, the note is where I left it. Inside, I unpack the few groceries and then have to get creative with making my coffee. I shake some beans into a clean sock, then twist the fabric forming a ball. Using the edge of my Leatherman, I smash the beans into a coarse ground. In one of the bottom cabinets, I find a lone stainless steel pot, fill it with water then boil it on the stove. In tiny increments, I pour the boiling water over the sock I've rested over a mug. The resulting brew is on the weak side with a slightly salty bite, but it gets the job done. While I'm turning over my laundry on the balcony, I hear a knock at the door.

I open it to find who I'm guessing is Silas. He's short and

gaunt, with grayish brown stubble covering his hollow cheeks and pointed chin. His eyes are a crystalline blue while the whites a yellow hue. Circular glasses about the size of half dollars rest on his thin nose. A derby hat is pulled tight over a thinning crop of hair that's the color and shininess of stained wood. He's wearing jeans, white low-top sneakers, and a jean jacket over a plain white tee. At his feet is a duffle bag almost as big as he is. Based on his size and the size of the bag, I'm not sure how he managed to get it here. An unlit cigarette dangles from his lips.

"Ezra?" he says.

"Yes."

"I'm Silas. You going to invite me in or what?"

"Sorry, yes. Please," I say. I point at the duffle bag. "Do you need a hand with that?"

"No," he says, dragging it into the apartment as if it were empty.

He drops the bag in the center of the room and gives the place a quick once over. Without asking, he lights his cigarette.

"So you want to know about IEDs?" he says, sending a gray puff of smoke into the air. "You've got the right guy. When do you ship out?"

"What's that?"

"Where you headed? The Middle East? Russia? Africa?"

"Oh," I say. "Sorry, here in the city is where I'm working."

Silas squints at me through the smoke.

"Here, huh? I'd heard rumors, but you know how it goes. It's hard to know what to believe anymore." He walks to the slider door and opens it wide. He taps his ash on the balcony and surveys the view as he talks. "I'd hoped they were just rumors. It's funny, really. That these supposed patriots are using the tactics of the guys we fought for decades." His gaze drifts off for a second, and then he glances over his shoulder. "What have you come across so far?"

"Grenades rigged to tripwires and ones that look like mortar rounds with a few wire attachments to them."

Silas nods and returns to his cigarette. "Yeah, those are some of the easier ones to make."

"I don't have much, but could I offer you something to drink?"

"You got any whiskey?"

"No. Sorry. Water or coffee is all I've got."

"I'll take a coffee if it's not too much of a hassle."

I set to fixing him a coffee. I'm a little embarrassed by how I have to make it, so I put my back to him and mash the beans as quietly as possible.

"Do you have any ideas of what else I might encounter?" I ask. "What should I watch out for?"

"Unfortunately, there's not a one size fits all manual for this type of thing. Especially if you're dealing with insurgents from a wide range of training backgrounds. Most of them don't know what the hell they're doing, so you see a lot of simple stuff like what you're describing. It really depends on how creative they get with it and how daring they are."

He scrapes the end of his cigarette against the balcony wall and sticks the butt in his pocket. From his jacket, he removes a pack of cigarettes and lights another.

"In the bag, I brought some documentation I had from back in the day. It'll give you a foundation of how most explosives work."

I filter the water through the beans, then hand him the mug. "I'll take whatever you've got."

"Are you on active duty? Or you serve in the past?" he asks.

"I never served."

"Never served, huh? Well, you must be dealing with some heavy shit if you're disarming bombs for the hell of it." He takes a sip of coffee and doesn't spit it out. "For me, I got a letter from my wife telling me my dog got run over and that she was leaving me for my cousin. Can you believe that? She put both of those things in one letter. After that, I didn't give a shit what happened to me for a long while." Silas sighs as he flicks the ash off his cigarette. He takes another drag, destroys the end on the wall, and puts the butt in his pocket. After another sip of coffee, he returns to the apartment and unzips the duffle bag.

"You're a bit bigger than me, but this might fit you still," he says as he takes out a heavy-duty-looking garment. "This is an EOD or bomb suit. Figured it might come in handy for what you're doing."

"Why do you have that?"

"Don't worry about the why or how. It's here and can help. That's all you need to know. Not many people go into this line of work, so if I find crazy enough bastards willing to do it, I help out where I can. A manual in the bag tells you how to put it on. The thing weighs a ton, and it gets hot as hell in there, so don't wear it for long stretches. It won't protect you from everything you can come across, but for small enough blasts, it can be the difference between living or dying."

The suit is olive green with black straps. I pick up the pants, then the main jacket section, feeling the heft. The whole suit is easily seventy to eighty pounds. I think it would be a logistical nightmare to transport this beast through the rubble alone, but if Silas could do it, I should be able to. Upon closer inspection, I see the duffle bag has wheels at the bottom and a rigid floor.

Silas extracts a thick binder from the bag.

"I've got a little time now, so I'll walk you through some essentials," he says.

Over three hours, he details how explosives work and things to watch out for. Each section he covers diverts to stories of his time in the Marines that seem unrelated to the topic. A rant about the country's current state follows the story; then, he falls silent with a far-off look before he moves on to the next issue. Silas stops talking when he's finished his pack of cigarettes. Staring into the empty pack, he stands and stretches.

"Well," he says, as he glances at his watch. "I should be on my way."

My head is swirling and overloaded with information, so part of me is glad the session has ended. I stand and offer my hand in thanks. He gives it a firm squeeze, then heads for the door. Out of his back pocket, he takes out a stack of papers. Swiping through them, he stops on a business card.

"Listen, I don't know you," he says, handing me the card. "But I know you if you follow me."

On the card is an organization name I don't recognize, with an address and a phone number.

Silas says, "You know there are groups for this kind of thing, brother. People to talk to. Help you see there's always something to live for, even if you think there isn't at the moment."

I nod and pocket the card. "I'll look into it."

He starts to walk away, then stops and comes back. "And if anyone should ever ask, I was never here."

I grin and nod again. Silas studies my eyes for a moment, then turns and disappears around a corner.

WEEK 10 - NOVEMBER 24

I take the rest of the day studying and digesting everything Silas told me. At night, I work on getting the blast suit on. It's cumbersome and challenging to get on by myself, but I finally secure it. I walk around the apartment, trying to acclimate to carrying the weight. It's apparent I need to get back into shape. In my prime, this would be no problem. I've walked maybe fifty yards, and I'm sucking wind. The suit, I decide, will only be used for complex situations that I don't feel confident in disarming. Otherwise, I'll go in exposed as I've been doing.

I wriggle out of the suit. The power cuts out again as I pack it into the duffle bag. Not tired yet, I decide to check out one of the Safety Zones following the tip the Dollar Tree worker gave me for getting meal replacement packs. I take my Leatherman and the Maglite and set off into the night. As I'm walking, my mind wanders to Isla. Guilt trickles into my heart that I haven't thought about her for a day or two. And what am I doing going to get sustenance? That's not the actions of someone looking to end it all and hopefully meet his love in the great beyond.

Part of me seems to be moving on like I'm disrespecting Isla's memory somehow. I should be home wallowing, suffering my loss, not out and about trying to live. What would she want for me? Is this it? Would she want me to move on? The consensus I've found over the years from others has been the deceased would want you to move forward. But would they? I try to imagine if the roles were reversed. I'd be dead, so I guess I wouldn't care one way or the other, but I try to think of Isla marrying someone new. The thought hurts a little, if I'm being honest. If she were happy, wouldn't that be what I wanted?

My mind drifts to the child Isla was carrying. I wonder if it would've been a boy or a girl? A girl would've been my preference. Sophia. Isabella. Penelope. Isla hated the name, Penelope. I'm sure if it were a girl, she would have been beautiful like Isla. I have to push the thoughts away as tears form. Stop thinking. Finish the task you set out to do right now. Focus on what's in front of you instead of what's behind you.

Forty-five minutes later, I arrive at the Saftey Zone in the northeast quadrant. A guard at the entrance scans my profile from my phone. Once it beeps me through, the guard asks, "Purpose of your visit?"

"I was told they're handing out free meal replacement packs here."

The guard taps something on his phone and points into the distance behind him.

"Building four," he says. "They'll need to run a finance check on you to see if you qualify."

My phone app leads me to building four. Three lines of people stand ten feet apart. At the end of each line is a table with two seated workers. Behind them are cargo trucks with the back gate opened. The line to the right has the fewest people in it, so I pick that one. When it's my turn, a young kid, not even in his twenties, looks at me with disdain in his eyes.

"I need your authorization to scan your financial accounts," he says.

"Why's that?" I say.

"To ensure your net worth meets the minimum threshold to receive support."

The kid rolls his eyes as if I should have known this information already. I hold out my phone, and he scans it. He studies a tablet for a few seconds, then taps another button. A guy standing at the truck reads his phone, selects two pouches from the shelves, and walks them over to the kid.

"Ok, you've been approved for a bi-weekly stipend for two pounds of M.R.P.," the kid says. "Each time you come back, you must have your finances scanned. Understand?"

Using a pen, the kid pushes the two pouches across the table for me to take.

"Next," he shouts to the person behind me.

I move out of the way and return to my apartment. When I enter, I test the light switch, but the power still isn't on. Using the Maglite, I glance over the pouches. They're black with the abbreviation for Meal Replacement Powder printed in a bold sans serif font on the front. The back lists the recommended water-to-powder ratios. I fill a glass with water until I am roughly where the instructions say I should be. The powder is a light tan with tiny red beads mixed in. A plastic scooping cup is inside the pouch, and I use it to dump two scoops into the water. After stirring the drink with a knife, I take a sip. The Dollar Tree girl wasn't kidding; it tastes like crap. I choke half of it down, then take a seat at the island. If I'm going to make it long enough to disarm as many bombs and mines as possible, I'll need some funds. Nothing crazy, just enough for the essentials. I pull up Evelyn's details and debate what to say to her. I feel like I'm fifteen again, trying to gather the courage to text a girl from class. Keep it simple. Keep it neutral is the approach I land on.

"If houses need mine clearing, I'm available," I say out loud as I type the message. As the message goes out into the ether, I relocate to the loveseat with my dinner in a glass. My phone vibrates, and I see that she's already responded. I wasn't sure she'd even get back to me, let alone respond so quickly.

The message says, "Great! Send me your profile, and I'll get you in the system."

I send her my details and then think of a way to bring up the financial end without coming across as desperate.

I type out, "I hate to ask, but were you able to secure funding?"

The three dots on the screen bounce as she types a response.

"Yes. Flat rate per building has been approved."

"Appreciated," I write back.

"When can you start?"

"Tomorrow."

"Perfect. I'll send you an app for download, and we can get started."

The following message she sends is a link for the app she referenced. I download it and go through the setup steps. Then I text her that I'm registered. A notification pops up in the app. When I open it, a map comes on screen with a dozen pins throughout the city. Another message comes through.

It says, "The map shows all the places that need clearing. I'll be at site six tomorrow morning by nine."

I tell her I'll be there, and she signs off with, "Get some rest."

With nothing else to do, I force down the rest of the M.R.P. drink, then head to the bathroom and brush my teeth with my finger. When I finish, I lie in bed, dozing off to thoughts of tripwires and bombs.

WEEK 10 - NOVEMBER 25

The following day I rise with the sun. After some light stretching, I mix another M.R.P. drink, grab Silas's binder, and head out to the balcony. There's enough sun reflecting off the surrounding buildings for me to skim over the notes. At eight, I take a minute-long cold shower, scrub my teeth, then get dressed. In the backpack Davis got for me, I load the binder, the roll of bubble wrap, the Maglite, and the headlamp. I leave the apartment and arrive at site six ten minutes early. To my surprise, Evelyn is already there, leaning against the wall, reading something on her phone. A scarf binds her hair, giving her a vintage '50s vibe like she could be ready for a drag race between Chevies. She's dressed in a sleek outfit that complements her long slender profile.

"Hello, there," I say.

She looks up and smiles. "Hi. Good to see you. Thanks for coming."

"Sorry, I wasn't expecting you to be here."

Her face goes apologetic. "Well, I kind of have to be here."

"You do?"

"Since funds are going towards this, I have to make sure you're actually here doing the job. And in case…in case…you know." With her hands, she makes a small explosion motion. And it makes sense to me, then. She has to be here in case I get killed.

"Ah," I say, scratching my beard. "I understand."

An awkward silence descends on us. Then Evelyn holds up her phone. "I can scan you in whenever you're ready."

"Sounds good."

She steadies her phone over mine. "Ok, you're all set. Like the first building, every room needs checking along with the stairwells. Digital keys are in your phone again. I'll be across the street." Her elegant finger points to a coffee shop four buildings down.

"Guess I better get to it then," I say.

"I'd say good luck, but that feels like it might be a jinx."

"That's fair," I say.

The building is straightforward. I don't find anything until the last floor. Another trip wire with a grenade. I disarm it and finish the sweep. Four hours have passed by the time I emerge into the afternoon sun. Evelyn spots me from the coffee shop and comes over.

"How'd it go?"

"One on the top floor. I didn't see anything else."

"Ok, good," she says as she takes out her phone. "Let me log it in quick. Then, I don't know, are you up for another one?"

I shrug and say, "Why not?"

She pans over the map, biting her lower lip as she does.

"There's a small building four blocks over. Site nine."

"Did you want to go ahead and meet me there?"

"What do you mean?"

"I just wasn't sure of your comfort level walking a foot away from someone with a grenade in their backpack."

"Oh," she laughs. "Right. I hadn't thought of that. Do you think it's safe?"

"The pin is taped closed, and I wrapped it in bubble wrap. Not that bubble wrap would contain a blast, but that's as safe as I know how to make it."

She considers this, shrugs, and says, "To hell with it. At least it'd give them something interesting to put on my headstone."

"That it would."

The walk is quiet for some time. Small talk wasn't my forte when times were good, so now I don't even know where to begin. She breaks the silence after a while.

"So, what were you before this?" she asks.

"I worked at Helios Solar doing installations and repairs. You?"

"A project manager at an ad agency. They said I could come back but I felt I could be more useful elsewhere."

"Makes sense."

"I can't believe it's Thanksgiving today. Doesn't feel much

like a holiday, does it?"

"All of the days just blur into one for me."

"I used to love Thanksgiving growing up. My mom was one of five children, so every year, aunts, uncles, and more cousins than you could keep track of packed our house. How about you? You got any family around?"

It's a logical question for someone trying to get to know a stranger. The words roll off her tongue with no hidden tone or meaning. It's a question I should have anticipated, but I didn't. I get a little flustered.

"I don't like to talk about that," I say.

"Oh, I'm sorry. I didn't..."

"I think I see the building up there."

I can't help the edge in my voice. She didn't do anything wrong and didn't deserve my attitude. But why should I get close to someone, even if it's just as a friend? If I have no one in my life, then I have no one else to lose. It's simpler that way. I need to keep what's left of my heart guarded. She is only a means to an end, and that's how I have to view her. A job needs doing. If I'm not here to do it, then who will?

We approach the building, and she takes out her phone. She avoids my eyes as she authorizes me for the site. "You're all set," she says. I brush past her without saying anything else. In the lobby of the building, I sit on the floor with my back to the wall, composing myself. It takes me twenty minutes to push the outside world's distractions from my mind. I go extra slow with my sweep and never take a break. I'm hoping Evelyn will have forgotten what a jerk I was if enough time goes by. I clear the place five hours later but probably could've done it in three. Two mortar IEDs are all that I find. At this point, I'm more afraid of facing her again than I am of the explosives.

After securing the mines in the backpack, I head outside. I don't see Evelyn, and I wonder if she went home. If she did, I wouldn't blame her. I get my bearings and decide to go to the river for disposal.

"All done?" Evelyn says.

I turn to see her behind me.

"Thought you might have left," I say.

"Nope. Need to make sure you're ok, remember?"

I nod and let her scan my phone.

"So what do you do with them?" she asks.

"I've been tossing them off the bridge over the river."

"Really?"

"If you have a better idea of where to get rid of them, I'm all ears."

Why? Just why? Stop being a prick. It's, unfortunately, easier said than done.

"I didn't mean it as a criticism," she says defensively. "Do you want a ride there?"

"I can walk."

"Listen," she says, grabbing my arm. When I look at her hand, she quickly retracts it. "I didn't mean to offend you by bringing up your family. I totally get it if you don't want to talk about it. I just figured if we're going to see each other for this job, I wanted to get to know you. If you want to keep it strictly to showing up and getting to it with no questions, we can."

"You don't want to get to know me. I can be dead tomorrow. Or you can. What's the point?"

Her face goes cold, and against the setting sun, her eyes look like pools of watercolors.

"I'm sorry you see it that way," she says. "Everyone has lost something in this war, you know. You're not special."

I grunt, then say, "You're right. I'm not special" And like that, I turn and walk away, leaving her alone in the shadows of the empty buildings.

Chapter 8

I lie awake in bed, staring at the ceiling. I can't sleep. Too many memories. Too many thoughts. I replay the conversation with Evelyn in my head again and again. You're not special. She cut to the core of me with three words. Isla would be disappointed at how I acted. Hell, I'm disappointed in myself. The guilt, anger, and shame keep me awake as if inconsolable newborns fill my room. Evelyn wanted to get to know me, and I didn't even give her a chance. What has she lost during this whole ordeal? I don't know because I've been too wrapped up in myself to ask. Selfish. Pathetic. What a waste.

I get out of bed and stumble to the balcony. Peering over the side, I can just make out the darkness of the pavement. Just do it. Get it over with already. Then someone with some value left can have this apartment you don't deserve. Then Evelyn won't have to bother being disappointed with what I can't give her.

But that's just being selfish, too. Running away like a coward. Too scared to face the world that's hurt me. And what about the rigged apartments? If I go now, how many others will suffer and die because I didn't help? I think of Davis then. What if he were to die from a mine that I could've disarmed? What would I tell Benson? Sorry, your grandson is dead. I'm just too self-absorbed. I slam my fist against the balcony railing.

"Coward," I whisper.

A gust of wind sweeps past with a familiar scent of Isla as if she is there with me.

"I'm sorry," I say to her. "I'm sorry. I miss you."

As tears overtake me and I sink to the floor, I know I need to apologize to Evelyn. Tired from the weight of emotions, I crawl back to the bed and drift off. When dawn breaks, I feel a little better. As I go through my morning routine, I rehearse my approach with Evelyn. I plan to message her around eight asking about the site we should meet at today. I'll keep the tone friendly. Then if she shows up, I'll apologize for being an asshole. I finish my M.R.P drink, then get dressed. Sitting on the loveseat, I text her.

"Morning. What site are we working on today?" I type.

She doesn't respond for close to an hour. When she does, the message states the site to meet at. No emojis or extra punctuation. I pull up the site on my phone and set off.

At the entrance to my building, a teenage girl stops me. Her clothes are dirty and tattered. Dirt is smeared across her face as if she's been crying. Cracks riddle her pale lips. She has ginger hair cut short with jagged edges. She's skinny to the point where it looks painful to move.

"Hey," she says, getting in my path and holding her hands out like two stop signs. "Are you the guy who does the...does...

the…the bomb work?"

Desperation floods her eyes. She moves around with jittery randomness as if she were a chicken being electrocuted.

"Easy," I say. "What's going on?"

"Please. Are you the guy? Are you the guy that does the bomb stuff?"

"My name's Ezra. Slow down and tell me what the problem is."

Her bony fingers dig into my forearm as she tries to drag me along with her. The attempt is like a chihuahua trying to drag a grizzly bear. I break the grip she has on me and take a step back.

"Please. You've got to help me. My friend… she's in trouble… she's going to die."

"What's happened to your friend?"

"We were just messing around. I dared her…I didn't know…I swear."

"I don't know what you're talking about. Take it from the top."

"We broke into one of the overtaken government buildings. The other kids told us it was closed because the government left along with the insurgents. We were just…I don't know…we were just trying to be cool and show them we weren't scared. We wanted to show them they were wrong."

"So why do you need me?"

"I dared her to go into a section cordoned off. It was stupid. I thought the signs were just bluffs to scare people. I didn't know…"

She trails off and has a distant gaze. Her eyes fill with tears.

"Hey, focus," I say. "What happened to your friend?"

"She's… she's trapped. I think it's one of those ransom mines. At least, that's what the other kids said it was. Bobby heard it on the news."

"Ransom mine?"

"Some sort of smart mine, that if someone steps on it, it arms a bomb. They blow up if they don't pay the ransom. If they step off the spot, it blows up. Bobby said they're impossible to disarm. You can do it, though, right?"

As the girl shakes like she's going to implode, I think of Evelyn and how she'll take me not showing up today. Some things, I guess, just aren't meant to happen.

"Show me where she is," I say.

The girl takes off running. She moves with an astonishing quickness for someone as frail as she is. I'm practically in a full-on sprint just to keep her in sight. After about a mile run, the girl stops in front of a government building in the city's center. She weaves through rubble and barriers, leading me to the rear of the building. Four teenagers in equally rough shape as the girl huddle around a dumpster shoved against a wall under a broken window. On top of the dumpster is a pallet that looks like a makeshift ladder to the window. Three of the other teenagers are boys, and the fourth is a girl. The biggest of the boys steps in front of the others as I come forward.

"This is the guy?" the big teen says. "He looks like shit, Sadie."

"I went to the address given to me," Sadie says. "He fit the description, and his name matched."

"Jesus, alright. She's in there," the big teen says, pointing to the broken window.

"Where inside?" I ask.

Sadie says, "Once you drop in, go right, then take the second left. You won't miss her. She's in the center at the top of the stairs."

I scale the Dumpster, test my weight on the pallet then climb up. At the ledge of the window, I peer inside. A decorative dresser is directly beneath the window. I straddle the ledge and can just get my foot onto the dresser. When I'm inside, I stop and let my senses acclimate to the new environment. The ceilings reach at least fifteen feet into the air. The floors are some sort of luxurious high polished stone that has taken on a matte texture from the ever-present dust of the city. Elaborate statues of eagles perch from light fixtures set at regular intervals. The place is dim, cast in a dull orange from the rising sun. I strain to pick up the hum of electricity but don't hear any. Power is either out or shut off while the place isn't in use.

After I get my phone light on, I walk down the hall to my right. If memory serves me, this building was part of the legislative branch of the government. I've never been inside before. The place is rather regal, and I'm sure it was a sight to see in its prime. I pass a series of thick dark stained wooden doors with brass knobs. At the second intersection, I turn left as instructed. The area I'm in is expansive. Its design gives me the impression this is the main entrance. Large glass double doors are on a lower level. Splitting off to the left and right are open curving stairs that lead to the next level where I am. The stairs connect to a narrow platform that branches into three hallways. I'm in the hallway to the left. In the center of the platform stands a girl.

"Hello," I say as softly as I can. I don't want to startle her. Her head lifts ever so slightly.

"Hello," she says. "Who's there?"

"My name is Ezra. Your friend, Sadie is it, came and got me. Said you might have stepped on a mine."

"She's not my friend," the girl rasps.

"I'm making my way to you now. It may take me a little bit,

so just hang tight."

I get down on all fours and sweep my light in steady even passes over the floor. A distance of maybe twenty feet separates us. The tile the girl is standing on is a two-foot square. A gap about the thickness of a coaster surrounds the tile and the one to its right. The tile itself sinks a half inch. I rise slowly and extend my leg over the adjacent tile to stand in front of the girl. She's young and scrawny like the other kids with similar battered clothing. Her eyes are a brilliant green that seems familiar.

"Hi," I say with a smile. "How are we doing?"

She lets out a short nervous laugh and says, "I've been better."

"So you think you stepped on a mine? Why do you think that?"

Her hand is shaking as she passes me her phone. The screen background is black. In the middle of the screen is a red warning symbol. Above the symbol is a message that reads, "Bomb armed. Move, and it will detonate. $500,000 needs to be transferred for deactivation." Beneath the symbol is a timer counting down. The timer has roughly three hours remaining.

"As soon as I stepped on the tile, my phone started going haywire. That was the message that came up. It had four hours originally," the girl says.

"Guess we better not waste any more time then."

"Where do these people think I'm going to get that kind of money? I'm just a kid."

"I don't think you were their intended target."

"Oh," she says. "Am I going to die?"

"I won't let that happen," I say. I'm surprised at how easily the lie rolls off my tongue. I have no idea if I can save her or disarm this bomb. If I can't, this will be the end for me, too. I know I wouldn't be able to live with this girl's death on my hands.

I inspect the floor, trying to work out where the explosives are. The tile next to her feels different. With the edge of my Leatherman, I tap lightly on the tile. A hollow sound thumps back. I tap a separate tile for comparison, and there's a clear sharper ring. Fake tiles are my best guess.

"I'm going below you to check something out," I say. "I'll be right back."

"Where are you going?" she says. Her eyes are wide with fear.

"I need to find where the explosives are. I want to see if I can access anything from the ceiling underneath you."

"Ok," she sighs.

I move down the stairs, taking the same precautions to avoid other hidden traps. Under the platform, the ceiling looks smooth. In a room off to the side, I find a chair. Standing on it, I can reach the ceiling. As I run my hands over it, I don't feel anything out of place. The insurgents could've gone in this way and patched it, but it seems unlikely. I don't have the tools or the time to go this way. So I return to the platform.

"Anything?" she asks.

"No. The tiles here, I think, are fake. I'm going to try and lift this one."

"What if it blows up when you try to mess with it? The other kids told me these things are like impossible to disarm."

"I'm going to go nice and slow. If it looks sketchy, I won't do it."

"Ok."

"What's your name by the way?"

"Harper."

"Harper. You look familiar. Do I know you?"

She searches my face for recognition, "I'm not sure."

"Where did you go to school?"

"Rand Elementary."

I remember now where I'd met this girl before.

"Rand," I say. "Mrs. Asher was your music teacher?"

"That's right," she smiles.

"I'm...I was...her husband. I carried you out of the school that day...when all this started."

She studies my face closer and I see recognition in her eyes.

"Oh yeah," she says. "You look different. Must be the beard."

"Yeah," I say, ruffling the scruff. "It's pretty bad, isn't it? When I get the chance and some extra cash, I need a serious shave."

"It looks itchy."

"It is, especially when it gets hot out."

I crouch next to the fake tile, then stretch onto my stomach. I unfold the knife blade and talk loudly, so Harper knows what I'm doing.

"Ok, I'm going to check now to see if wires or blockages might be attached to the tile."

I pick an entry point and slip the blade in. Slowly I pull it towards me, feeling for any type of resistance. All four sides seem smooth.

"I don't feel anything. I'm going to try and pop this tile off now."

Harper nods. I come to my knees for leverage. I jimmy the knife at an angle and gradually apply downward pressure until I hear a pop and the edge of the tile comes free. With my light, I do another inspection underneath to see if I can spot any other wires. None are visible, so I set down the Leatherman and work my fingers under the edge. I lift the tile as if I'm in a bucket of glue. No snags tugging on it so far. When the tile is free, I do one more check underneath before setting it aside.

I peer into the hole and my stomach drops. The device inside looks like something from the future, with wires jutting out from the central unit. Lights with different colors line the edge. Some of the lights are solid, while others are blinking. My face must show what I feel because Harper asks, "What's wrong?"

"Uh, well, let's just say this looks like a professional job."

"Oh my god, I'm going to die. I'm going to die."

"Easy. Let's not get ahead of ourselves."

"You think you can stop it?"

"I'm not sure yet. Give me a second."

Whoever made this setup knew what they were doing. It's a far cry from the mines I've encountered in the other buildings.

"I'll be right back."

I retrace my steps to the window where I came into the building. The teenagers are still there. Sadie is sitting on the Dumpster.

"Hey," I call to them. "Listen closely. I need you all to go back to my apartment. Imprint your finger, and I'll send you the code to get in. Inside you'll find a large duffle bag. I need you to bring that here. It's heavy, so you'll all need to help. Bring it to the front of the building, and I'll let you in."

"Is she ok?" Sadie says.

"She won't be if you don't hurry."

They look at each other, debating what to do.

"Does one of you have a phone?" I ask.

One of the boys raises his hand.

"Give me your number," I say. The boy recites it while I input it into my phone. "Alright, better get going. We don't have a lot of time."

"I'm on it," Sadie says, then hops off the Dumpster and takes off running. The others hesitate before running after her. With that done, I hustle back to Harper.

"Your friends…sorry…the others are going to go get some stuff for me that I think can help."

"That's good," Harper says.

"How are we looking on time?"

She glances at her phone, "Two hours and nine minutes."

While I wait for the other kids to bring the gear, I scrutinize the bomb more, seeing if I can piece together what might do what.

"What happened to Mrs. Asher?" Harper asks.

"What do you mean?"

"You said you were her husband. Did you guys get divorced?"

I pull back from the bomb and sit on the floor, bending my knees towards my chest.

"No," I say.

"Is she gone?"

I stare at my hands and nod.

"That's too bad," Harper says. "She was my favorite teacher. She was really nice and told funny jokes and taught us all about film scores, which was pretty cool."

"Yeah," is all I can say without breaking into tears. It's weird how the slightest memory can change my mood in the blink of an eye. I can't break down in front of this girl. I need to stay stable to get her out of this mess. "Your parents still around?"

"No, but not because of the fighting. They've been gone a long time. I never really knew them. My mom left after I was born. I don't know if she's alive or dead. I never met her. My dad drank himself to death. He's been gone for six years now."

"Who do you live with then?" I ask, glad to be turning the conversation away from Isla.

"I bounce around. I was with my grandmother for a while, then she died. Then a distant aunt and uncle, but they sucked, so I left. Been in an orphanage for the last two years."

She talks about her life with humility and candor far beyond her age. An old soul.

"How'd you end up here?" I ask.

"Since all the schools have been closed, a bunch of kids like me roam around the city. The older kids dared Sadie and me to come in here. I've got this problem where I can't back down from a dare. So, here I am."

I grin, "I can respect that."

She shifts uncomfortably and bites her lower lip.

"I'm sorry, but I have to ask. It's super embarrassing, so please don't laugh."

"What's up?"

"I have to pee so bad. I've been holding it for the past hour, and it's killing me."

"Oh," I say, standing. "Let me see what I can do."

I roam around for a little, checking the conference rooms, and spot a vase with shriveled flowers inside. I dump the contents and search another room, an office, by the looks of it. There's a box of tissues on a desk that I snatch.

"This should work," I say, holding up the items like a hunting dog retrieving pheasants. I'm about to hand the vase to her but stop.

"What?" she says.

"I don't know if the extra weight will affect the bomb's trigger mechanism. Obviously, if you get off it, it'll explode, but I don't know about the reverse."

"That's a thing?"

"I'd hate to risk it. When the kids get here with my stuff, I have some documents I can review to see if that can happen. I'm just unsure about the sensitivity of the trigger you're on."

"So what am I supposed to do?"

I shrug with a frown.

"I'll have to hold the vase."

"Oh, man. Are you serious?" she groans.

"I mean, how bad do you have to go?"

"Guh, ok. I just don't care. Don't look, though."

"I won't," I say. "Um, alright, well, I guess I'll position it in the general direction, then you just guide me into place when you're ready."

"This is so embarrassing," she says. "You couldn't find something bigger?"

"For someone about to burst, you're awfully picky." Then I remember seeing a wastebasket in the office where I got the tissues. "Hold on." I replace the vase with the basket and show it to Harper. "Will this do?"

"That's much better."

"Ok. Ready?"

I bend my knees and hold the bucket in the ballpark where the stream will flow. With my free hand, I cover my eyes and turn my head away from her.

"You sure you're not looking?"

"Listen, this isn't my idea of a good time either."

She grumbles again, and then I hear her undoing her pants. Her hand guides mine into position. A few seconds later, she starts to pee. When she finishes, I keep my hand over my eyes and take a few steps back.

"Alright, you can look now," she says.

I drop my hand from my eyes and put the bucket in a hall out of the way. When I return, Harper doesn't look at me as she whispers, "Thanks."

"Think nothing of it. I've dealt with worse," I say. "My

buddy has four kids. When we met his second kid, he and his wife thought it'd be funny if I changed the kid to get practice. The kid peed all over me. Some of it even hit me in the face."

"Ugh," she laughs. "That's nasty."

"I think some even got in my mouth."

She laughs again, "You're full of it."

"Maybe a little."

My phone buzzes then with an alert. The teens made it to the apartment. I forward the entry code to the boy's phone. He texts me that they're inside and found the bag.

"Time check," I say.

Harper says, "One hour and fifty minutes."

I do the math in my head. The trip took them about twenty minutes to get there. Let's say it takes them thirty to return, accounting for the weight of the bag, which leaves me roughly eighty minutes to figure out how to disarm the explosive. It'll be tight.

"Ok, those guys are in my apartment and should be back here soon," I say.

"Good, because I don't think I can stand much longer. My knees are killing me."

"Here," I say, shuffling behind her. I sit down, careful to keep my body away from the tile but as close as I can to Harper. I bring my knees to my chest. "You can rest on my back. Don't take your weight off the tile, but you can at least bend your knees a little to take some of the pressure off."

"Are you serious?"

"Yes. Don't need you dropping when the end is in sight."

"Uh, ok," she says. "I guess for a little. If it is too much, just tell me to get off."

Her hands probe behind her, touching my shoulders to

feel where I am. Then she eases against my shoulder blades. I barely feel her there.

"Better?" I ask.

"Better," she sighs with relief.

I want to keep her mind distracted, hell, mine too. Thankfully, she's easy to talk to. "So, did you have a favorite film score?"

"Hmmm," she says. "I'd say anything by John Williams. I also like cello stuff a lot with inspiration from Asian styles. What about you?"

"I'm a big John Barry and Eric Serra fan. The old stuff is the best in my opinion. Nothing quite compares these days."

"It's funny. I never thought about movie scores until Mrs. Asher's classes. When I watch movies now, I sometimes notice the scores more than the movie. How do you think someone becomes a movie composer?"

"I'm not sure, to be honest. Study a lot of music, I guess. Then learn how to write it."

"That'd be a pretty cool job."

"I imagine it would."

Harper's quiet for a moment, then asks, "How did Mrs. Asher die?"

I let out a long sigh, then say, "A missile strike."

She's quiet again, then says, "Do you miss her?"

"Yeah. A lot. And days when I don't, I get mad at myself."

"Why?"

"I don't know. I guess...I don't want to forget her. If I don't think about her, I feel like I'll just keep losing more of her."

"I understand."

Being in this girl's presence puts things in perspective. I feel foolish for what I've admitted to her. She's lost just as much, if not more, than I have. I got to be with Isla for almost two decades, and she only got a few measly years with her parents. If anyone has been cheated, it's her.

"Do you think we see people we've lost when we die? I don't mean in Heaven or that crap, but like someplace humans can't see. Like a different radio frequency or a pitch that we can't hear. You know how dogs can hear things we can't? So maybe there's a place where part of us still exists after we die."

"Anything is possible. Plenty we still don't understand about this world. You don't believe in Heaven?"

"Nah, that's too sappy. Religion is all made up anyway."

I laugh, "I'm with you on that."

We sit in silence for a bit longer. Her warmth and steady breathing almost lull me into sleep. Then tapping on glass catches my attention.

"What's that?" Harper says.

"Hopefully, my gear is here," I say. "Ease yourself back up, and I'll check it out."

Once she's off my shoulders, I move to the platform's railing and see the teens peering through the front doors. Before letting them in, I check for any additional traps. Sadie greets me.

"We got it," she says, standing aside for me to see the others holding the duffle bag.

"Perfect." I take the handles on the bag from them and lug it inside. "Can you stay close if I need you for anything else?"

Sadie nods. "We'll be across the street."

"You did well. Thank you."

She smiles, then I watch as they scatter from the building. I manhandle the bag up the steps and set it down. Beneath the blast suit, I find the binder of information from Silas.

"What's all that?" Harper says.

"Information. I think I saw something in here the other night about this type of setup."

I place the binder near the hole and flip through the contents, skimming for anything resembling the bomb.

"How are we doing with time?"

"An hour ten left."

Sweat is forming at the base of my neck. I stop on a page that looks promising. As I compare what's in the manual with what's in the hole, I notice too many inconsistencies. More pages go by with nothing useful. There's a page on wiring that I study for a bit, but the seconds ticking away are ever-present at the back of my mind, and it makes it hard to focus on the words. I'm wasting precious seconds. I get to the end of the manual and double back to the start. Her phone doesn't even make a sound, but I hear tick, tick, tick in my ear. I close my eyes and scroll through everything I've ever learned about electricity and wiring. None of it gives me confidence in manipulating the device in front of me. I was stupid to think I could do something like this. Stupid to have lied to this poor girl. When my eyes open, I realize I don't have the skills to disarm this bomb.

WEEK 10 - NOVEMBER 26

How am I going to break the news to this poor girl? How can I tell her I failed? She has an entire life ahead of her, but now she won't get to live it. There's got to be a way. Think. Think, god damn it.

"Is something wrong?" she asks with a tremble she's trying to hide.

I stare at her and shake my head in disgust at myself. "I don't think I can disarm this. I just...I just don't know enough to risk it."

"Oh," she whispers, fighting back the tears.

"I'm going to get you out of here."

"Just go. This is all my fault. You shouldn't get hurt because of it."

"I'm not leaving you," I say, stepping in front of her. "Look at me."

She reluctantly does.

"I'm not leaving you," I shout. "You're going to live a long life and do everything you want to do. Understand?"

With the tips of her fingers, she wipes away a few tears.

"I'm sorry for yelling. I'll... I'll figure something out."

I pace to the top of the stairs, sizing up the room with fresh eyes. If I could put myself on the tile, I'd willingly do it. I just don't know what that would do to the trigger having extra weight on it. There are two wires I could cut, but this isn't something you can be anything but a hundred percent on. My eyes travel to the duffle bag and the blast suit. What could I do with that suit? I could cut the wires with it on, but if I'm wrong, Harper's dead, and I probably still would be too. I put my hand on the rail, thinking. As I do, my gaze follows the rail up to Harper. Squeezing the rail, an inkling of an idea comes to me. I take a few steps down and gauge the distance from the platform to the lower level. About ten to fifteen feet, I estimate. It just might work.

"How much time do we have?" I ask Harper with urgency.

"Fifty-one minutes."

I hurry down the stairs and burst out the front door. When I spot the teens, I wave for them to come to me. They don't waste any time crossing the street.

"What is it?" Sadie says.

"I need you guys to try and find something soft like a

mattress. Doesn't matter the quality. As many as you can find.
Just anything that's bigger than me and can cushion a fall.
And it needs to be done in forty minutes. Do you think you
can do it?"

They exchange glances, each genuinely seeming to think
of where they could find something. One of the boys says,
"There's a shelter a block over with beds. They might let us
take one or two of them."

"They won't believe us," another girl sneers.

"They might," the boy fires back.

"Don't be an idiot," the girl says.

"What about that FedEx on Fourth St?" Sadie says. "It took
a lot of damage during the fighting, but there might be pack-
aging supplies in there that we could use."

"It's worth a shot. Try both. But you need to be back here
in forty minutes," I say.

There are a few more grumbles with this request, but they
set off anyway. I pop my head back into the building and shout
to Harper.

"I'll be back in just a minute. Hold tight."

She shouts something, but I'm already outside to hear what
she says. I sprint up a block and look both ways in search of
the nearest pile of debris. From all the bombings, I don't have
to search far. I dig around until I find a piece of loose metal
about double the length of my arm. The bar is heavy as hell,
but that's what I need. I heave it onto my shoulders and stagger
back to Harper.

"What's that for?" she asks as I trudge up the stairs.

"Plan B."

I set the bar down in front of her. The railing comes up
to her waist. Round spires a little thicker than Harper's leg

are evenly spaced out and support the handrail. Designers implemented 3D printing to make the railing look like stone. 3D printing typically was a cheaper option, and seeing as this is a newer government building, I'm betting on them cutting costs wherever possible. I slip the bar through two spires so one end rests on the platform overhang. With the other end, I push it until it meets the handrail, creating a lever.

"Cover your eyes," I tell Harper. "I don't want anything flying off and hitting you in the face."

"What are you trying to do?"

"If I can get this railing off, well... we're going to jump."

"Jump?"

"I'm going to wear the blast suit and dive off with you in front of me. The explosion should radiate up while we're falling. Anything from the blast should be absorbed into the suit, protecting you."

By the expression on Harper's face, I can tell she thinks I'm insane. She glances over the railing. "That's a decent fall, isn't it?"

"We'll see what that gang of yours turns up with. If they can't find anything, we'll have to risk it. The fall might hurt like a son of a bitch, but we should survive it."

"What if the bomb blows up the whole building?"

"I don't think it's that type of bomb. I think it'd have to be a lot bigger, and there's not a lot of room in that hole. They wouldn't need something to level the building if they used it to ransom a single person. Theoretically, anyway."

Harper looks at the hole in the floor, then over the rail again, then at me.

"This is nuts, right?" she says.

"It is, yes, but it's the best I've got right now."

She inhales deeply, exhales through her nose, and whispers, "Ok."

I spread my legs and flex my knees. I don't want to create too many vibrations through the floor, so I start by resting the bar on my shoulder and pressing. The rail doesn't give an inch. I relocate the end of the bar to my hands and give a short, powerful strike into the rail, trying to focus as much energy on it as possible. After the first strike, I stop and listen to ensure nothing is disturbed by the explosive. Nothing gives me an indication that there's a problem, so I strike it two more times. On the fourth strike, I hear a distinct cracking sound of material separating. I get back into the lever pose and give it everything I've got. The bar feels like it's crushing bones in my shoulder, but I ignore the pain and keep going.

"Come on, you bastard," I shout and give it one last shove.

The section of the rail splits, and the bar shoots through. I stop myself from going over the side with it. I remove the bar and repeat the process in the next section. It breaks apart much easier now, with its structural integrity weakened. When I break enough of it, I set the bar aside and kick each section, sending them to the lower level. Then I go down and do a bare-bones job of clearing the debris.

"Time?" I say.

"Thirty-nine minutes."

While on the lower level, I pop outside quickly and scan the vicinity for the teens. I don't see them, so I go back and unpack the blast suit. As I'm laying all the pieces out, I can tell the weight will be a problem with getting out of the direct line of the blast quickly. The pants, I decide, will be left behind. It will leave my legs exposed, but at least my vital organs will get some protection. From what I remember from trying the suit on, I had enough mobility in my arms to be able to grab Harper.

I hear movement below, then Sadie shouts.

"We've got some stuff."

She and another girl hold a box taller than them. Pink-packing peanuts fill the box to the brim. The box is three feet deep, it probably won't do much, but it's a start.

"Bobby texted me and said they were able to get a mattress. He said it's really heavy, though, so it's taking them a while to get here."

"Can you take me to them?" I ask.

"Yeah," Sadie replies.

"Good. Both of you come with me." I look at Harper. "We're in the home stretch."

We find the boys a block over, struggling with the mattress. They're in the process of tipping it end over end to move it. Both of the boy's faces are red and drenched in sweat. I grab the front end, hoist it, and then shout commands to the rest.

"The three of you grab the back end. You, once we have it raised, go underneath and support the middle. We need to haul ass."

Everyone gets into position, and our combined forces allow us to make up ground. We get into the building and chuck the mattress into place. I eyeball the spot where I think we'll land. The box of packing peanuts gets centered on the mattress.

"Time?"

"Thirteen minutes," Harper says.

"You guys get out here," I say to the teens. "Call an ambulance and tell them to get here as soon as they can."

They linger for a moment, staring at Harper.

"Go," I shout at them, then I run up the stairs.

I rip some tissues out of the box and hand them to Harper.

"Roll these up and stuff them in your ears. This is going to be quick. Soon as I have the suit on, I'm going to run at you. Don't jump. Just let me take you off of the tile."

Her gaze is a million miles away.

"Harper," I say, waiting until she locks on my eyes. "This is almost over. We're going to get out of here."

She nods.

"Let me hear the words," I say.

"We're going to get out of here," she says.

"Good."

I stuff some tissue in my ears, then get on the top half of the blast suit. The last piece is the helmet. Once it's all on, I swing my arms around and sprint down a short hall to get a feel for the weight. It's top-heavy and not easy to maneuver. I only need to do this once, though. Make it count.

"Ok, are you ready?" I shout.

Harper gives me a thumbs up. I angle myself, so I'm on a direct path to grab her and go straight off the platform. My heartbeat is thundering inside the helmet. This is it. No more thinking. I lean forward and run.

The weight of the suit wants to pull me to the ground. I force my head back to keep myself upright. My eyes dart to Harper, then to the tile. The distance between us is closing. When I'm five feet from her, I focus on planting my left foot right before the tile she's standing on without touching it. My arms go wide. Harper closes her eyes and puts her arms tight to her sides. Her body is tense in anticipation of the impact. I push off and barrel into her, making sure I keep her as covered as possible. Her body slams into my chest, and my arms close in one fluid motion. My right foot lands just past the tile, and

I use it to propel us forward.

In the first second that she's off the tile, I don't hear or feel anything. And in that second, I wonder if the bomb wasn't actually active. Maybe it was a bluff. But in the next second, the thought is wiped away. The bomb erupts. A deafening boom tears through my ears despite the helmet and the tissues. The shockwave shoves me in the back. As we're falling, I rotate my body as far as I can, trying to land on my side, so I don't crush Harper once we hit the ground. Then I feel something searing hot hit my left leg just below my knee. The heat sends a lightning bolt of pain straight to my brain. Everything up to this point is in slow motion. Then in an instant, time seems to go into warp speed. The ground rushes forward, and we crash into the packing peanuts, creating an explosion of our own. Our combined weight bores through the packing peanuts like a bullet through a piece of paper. My shoulder hits first. Another burst of pain rips through my nervous system as we come to a stop.

Pieces of tile and debris rain down from the platform. I shield Harper's face from the flying bits with my free arm. I stay in the position until I don't feel anything else hitting us. Smoke drifts through the room. A distant hum rings in my ears. I lay there a little longer, allowing everything to settle. Then I lift my arm and check on Harper. Her eyes are shut, and a stream of blood comes from her nose.

"Harper," I say.

With my hearing messed up, I can't tell if I'm shouting. I work my damaged arm free from under Harper and gently rest her limp body on the mattress. A blinding pain shoots through my leg as I try to sit up. Blood soaks the pant leg. Something wedges deep into the flesh, but there's so much blood I can't tell what it is. I try to raise my right arm to help get the helmet off, but I can barely lift it. Dislocated shoulder, maybe. Collar bone doesn't feel right, either. Using my left hand, I fumble with the latches and manage to remove the helmet.

"Harper," I repeat as I nudge her arm. "Harper. Are you ok?"

She doesn't respond, and I can feel my chest tightening.

"Harper, please," I say, shaking her more forcefully. "Come on, kid, wake up."

This isn't happening. All of my fears and failings bubble to the surface. I want to give up. I want to scream. She can't be dead. She can't be. While I'm spiraling, the rational part of my brain chimes in. A pulse. Feel her neck; my mind prods me. Check for a pulse. As I'm about to touch Harper's skin, my vision splits her into three versions of herself. I can't focus. Warmth floods my stomach, and a fuzzy black ink creeps in from the outer rim of my eyes. She's so still and almost peaceful looking. That's the last thought I have before blacking out.

Chapter 9

I'm floating in a void. It's the same sensation of being in that weird limbo space between a dream and reality. I'm aware of myself in an ethereal kind of way, but at the same time, I don't know where I am. In the next instant, I'm in a forest with trees so big they must have been growing since the dawn of time. The forest is dark, but it's not nighttime. Everything I can see is a rich hue of green and brown. Tiny slits of blue sky peek through the dense foliage. A bird banks around one of the trees and lands in front of me at my feet. A robin. It's not afraid of my presence. It chirps and bobs its head, then takes flight, settling on a branch next to my face. The chirping continues as if it's talking to me in a language I once knew when man was new and more in tune with nature. The robin flies to another branch and chirps again. I follow the bird to the next tree. From there, the bird ascends to a large branch about twenty feet off the ground. It speaks to me in its ancient tongue, telling me to keep following her. The branches are thick and strong, so I have no problem scaling them.

When I reach the branch that the robin has stopped on, I straddle the limb and rest my back against the tree. The robin hops to the edge of a nest with three lightish blue eggs. One of the eggs wiggles and then cracks. As the shell gives way, a small feathery head emerges, struggling its way into the world. I blink, and the nest is gone. I peer at the ground to see if it fell off but don't see anything. Then I feel something move in my hand. Sitting in my palm is another robin. With my index finger, I pet its head. The robin closes its eyes, seeming to enjoy my touch. For some reason, I suddenly want to cry, but not in a sad way. The bird chirps, but instead of hearing a chirp, I hear my name. It's faint and delicate as if the wind carried it to me. The robin turns and then flies off without a goodbye, disappearing into the forest.

Then I wake up.

The light against my eyes causes them to water as I try to move my hand to wipe the moisture away; something tugs at the vein in my arm. I tilt my head and see an IV running to a fluids pouch. Sticking out of my nose is a small tube. I try to remove the tube with my other arm, but a sling keeps it in place. My eyes adjust to the brightness of the lights, and I can tell I'm in a small hospital room. A monitor to my left displays my vitals. As the grogginess fades, I'm aware of an odd sensation running through my leg. I attempt to kick the blankets away. My left leg doesn't respond to the command my brain gives it. The lack of control causes me to panic. I hear the monitor with my vitals beeping. A nurse rushes into the room.

"My leg doesn't feel right," I tell her.

"Yes, I understand," she says while pressing some buttons on the monitor. Then a warm wave flows through my blood, and sleepiness overcomes me. When I come to, a man who I assume is the doctor is studying a tablet next to the bed. The same nurse that put me to sleep is by his side.

"Hello there, Ezra," the doctor says as if he's known me my whole life. "I'm Dr. Washington, and this is nurse Belham." He motions to the nurse. She's medium height and slightly overweight, in her early thirties, with auburn hair and matching eyes. The doctor is older, late fifties, with dark skin, short hair, and a combination of a kind face and smile. He pushes thick transparent framed glasses to a better position on his nose.

"You're at the Northwest campus of the Sanders Hospital. The paramedics got you here just in time. You're lucky to be alive."

"My leg... doesn't feel right...."

"This won't be easy to hear," Dr. Washington clears his throat and speaks with sympathy, "We found a piece of shrapnel lodged in your left leg. It did substantial damage, and unfortunately, it was beyond repair. We had to amputate below the knee. However, we were able to make a successful fusion of a state-of-the-art prosthetic that utilizes robotics. Through rehab and practice, you should be able to walk unassisted again in no time."

I stare at my leg covered by the sheet, letting the words sink in. I'm missing a part of my leg under there. I wonder if I'm still in some sort of a dream. When I don't respond, Dr. Washington continues.

"You also suffered a dislocated shoulder and had a hairline fracture in your collarbone. Both seem to be healing nicely. We noticed minor damage to your eardrums. If it becomes a problem for what you can hear, we can get you fixed up with a hearing aid."

"How…how long have I been here?"

"Just over three months. Now that you are awake, we can get you going with rehab. In maybe a month or so, you should be able to leave and go back to your life."

Life? I'm not sure what life he's referring to. I think of Harper, then.

"What happened to the girl?" I ask.

"I'm sorry, what girl?"

"The girl I was with. Harper. Is she ok?"

"I don't know of any girl by that name. I deal with surgeries. She would've gone somewhere else in the hospital if she didn't require one. Do you have a last name? We can check the system and see if she's here."

I realize I don't know her last name or if she's even alive. Helplessness overcomes me. My heart sinks that I won't know what happened to her. I scrub through the memories of that day, trying to focus on any signs of life I saw in her. Did I see her move? A flicker of an eyelid? Anything? I hold the thoughts for a little longer, but there's too much fog to see clearly.

"I don't know her last name," I say. "She was young, under twelve. Green eyes. Skinny. I need to know if she's alive or not."

Dr. Washington and the nurse exchange a look, then he says, "We'll see what we can do. In the meantime, let's try and get you up and moving, and we'll go from there. If you need anything, press the button."

He gives me a reassuring smile, then leaves the room. Nurse Belham steps forward, studies the monitors, and checks my vitals.

"What's your pain level on a scale of one to ten?" she asks.

I want to tell her to pick the highest number she knows

and double it. The type of pain I feel can't be quantified. So I say, "Seven."

"Would you like to try standing up?"

"Ok."

She rolls the sheet down, and my breath catches in my throat at the sight of my leg. Below the knee is a rounded, heavily bandaged stump. Attached to it is a contraption that looks like it came straight from a science fiction movie. Metal rods, pistons, and wires weave down through the artificial shin into an equally metal foot. A flat screen embedded in the side of the limb towards my knee glows to life, showcasing intricate data.

"Inside is an extremely advanced computer," nurse Belham says. "It utilizes artificial intelligence and can compensate for how you walk. So the more walking you can do, the sooner it will learn how to move and balance you out. It will take some getting used to, and the other muscles in your leg will eventually adapt. I'll be honest with you, there's going to be some pain as you get started, but we can manage that for you."

She lowers the arm of the bed and moves the IV out of the way.

"We'll do something short, just to the door and back. Ready to give it a try?"

I let out a sigh and nod.

"Ok, I'll help you get your legs off the bed. Then I want you to sit there for a bit to get used to being more vertical again. Then we'll have you stand, wait a bit, and then if you're good, we'll take a few steps."

Moving just to the edge of the bed is an event. Every muscle and bone in my body rebels at the disturbance of their slumber. I feel the blood rushing to my head. She helps me out of the sling, gives my shoulder a light massage, and then works it in gentle sweeping motions. It's stiff, but I can move it much easier than I could right after the blast. Once a few minutes sitting there go by, nurse Belham says, "Ready?"

"Sure."

She takes my hand and braces herself so that I can use her as a crutch. My good foot touches the ground, and the robotic one goes next.

"Now, as slow as you can, ease your weight down," nurse Belham says.

When I do, a throbbing ache radiates around the intersection of the metal and flesh.

"You ok?" she asks, watching my face for signs of passing out.

All I can do is grunt, as talking would take too much concentration. She guides me into taking two steps. A soft whirring noise comes from the limb as the computer and pistons kick into gear. We make the trek to the door and back. I sink into the bed, exhausted.

"That was excellent," she says. "I'll give you something for the pain now so you can sleep, and the real work will begin tomorrow."

As she raises the bed rail, her hand lingers momentarily, and I place mine on top of hers.

"Please, if you find her...I just want to know what happened. Good...or bad," I say.

Nurse Belham searches my eyes for a moment, then says, "Her name is Harper?"

"That's right."

She smiles, "I'll do my best."

"Thank you," I say, letting the pain medications pull me into sleep.

WEEK 24 - MARCH 2

Not knowing what happened to Harper is slowly eating away at me. I can feel myself falling back into the state of despair I was in after Isla died. It'd be so easy to slip back into that lifeless existence. To not care. To give up. But I have to keep going until I know that Harper's dead or alive. That slice of hope shoves me forward. I resolve to get better as soon as I can. If she's still alive and I get the chance to meet her again, I don't want her to see me like this. The fighting, losing Isla, losing the child, losing my home. It was all so senseless. Being here in this hospital needs to have meant something.

The first week of rehab is the hardest, but I stay determined and do whatever the doctors tell me. They gradually start weaning me off of the pain meds. I eat the bland food they give me. I do the stretches. I pour everything I have into rehab and learn my new leg's ins and outs. There are days my whole body hurts, and I want to quit, but I don't. I keep moving and keep my mind busy. By the end of the second week, I'm getting around better, and the computer built into the limb continually improves the response and functionality based on my movements. The device is truly incredible. I ask nurse Belham daily for any updates on Harper, and every day, she gives me a frown with no news. Some days I think she avoids me to escape my incessant questions. I can't fault her for it. I'm a good patient, which is the only reason I think she tolerates me.

Belham is walking beside me, leading me back to my room, and she says, "You're making excellent progress. I think next week we might be able to discharge you. Any thoughts about what you'll do?"

"I'm not really sure. Maybe become a marathon runner."

She laughs at the joke. "You were in solar, right? The city

is reopening a lot of sectors, and I see job postings for people with your skill set all the time. I'm sure you could get into that again with no problem."

"Maybe," I shrug. I've considered this before, but it reminds me of my old life, and I'm not sure that I want to be reminded of that every day I go to work. To truly move forward, I feel like I'd need to start new. The prospect is both terrifying and exciting.

"Well, I'm sure you'll figure it out."

WEEK 25 - MARCH 11

A Friday rolls around. After five o'clock dinner, I head up to the hospital's eighth floor, where they have a sort of park that juts out from the main structure of the building. Trees line the perimeter's two walls, and a pond is in the center. The wall opposite the entrance to the park is left open and overlooks the city. There's a bench off to the side that sits under an oak tree, giving me an unobstructed view. I've claimed the spot as my own. The air is cool yet pleasant, and the sun bathes the city in a soothing glow of gold and dark shadows. From the little news I've been watching, the government restored electricity, and construction crews have been trickling in to help clean up. Specific sectors have already been slated for reconstruction. Like my leg, the city will need time to heal. For the first time in a long while, a shred of tentative optimism seems to be the throughline.

Nurse Belham comes into view and approaches me.

"Time to head back in already?" I ask, not wanting to return to my room yet.

She smiles, "No. You've actually got a visitor."

"A visitor?"

Nurse Belham hands me a tablet. On the screen is a news article from a local outlet. The headline reads, 'Hero saves girl from ransom mine'. As I scroll down the screen, a photo of myself appears. It's my ID photo from Helios. My heartbeat quickens as I come to the next shot. It's a posed picture of Harper sitting on a building stoop, smiling. Her full name, Harper Shaw, is written out in the photo's caption.

"You should have told me you were famous," Belham says as I look up from the screen, confused. "That would've made things a lot easier."

I'm about to ask her a question when I hear a voice.

"Hello, Ezra."

I glance over my shoulder and see a young girl standing a few feet away. I don't recognize her until I see her green eyes.

Harper.

I stand and face her, unable to move. The familiar pressure in my throat that I feel right before I'm about to cry is present. Harper floats towards me, transformed. She's still skinny but looks to have gained some weight. Her hair is clean and glimmers in the sun. A light layer of blush and mascara adorns her face. She's wearing a hip graphic patterned dress under a light gray jacket. A pristine pair of white shoes and a small purse slung over her shoulder complete the look. As she draws closer, I'm thinking of something to say, but my mind's gone blank. I can see tears in her eyes as she takes a step, then throws her arms around my stomach, pulling me into a tight hug. My arms close around her as I shut my eyes to keep the tears at bay.

She presses back and says, "I'm happy you made it."

I can barely breathe. "Ditto," I choke out.

Nurse Belham smiles at me as she slips away. I hold my

hand toward the bench, and Harper and I sit. There are so many things I want to say. So many things to ask. I start simple.

"How...how have you been?" I ask.

"Been a crazy few months."

"Were you hurt badly from the fall?"

"They treated me for a concussion and a few bruised ribs. The fall knocked me unconscious. My hearing was jacked up for a while. Other than that, they said I was ok. I was in the hospital for only a few days."

"Good... that's good. And what about these clothes? A far cry from when we met."

She looks at the dress and then at her hands. "So all those kids with us talked you up to anyone that would listen. Told everyone what happened...what you did. A journalist tracked me down and wrote a story on the whole thing. Interviewed me and whatnot. So when you get out of here, they'll probably want to talk to you."

"Me? Why?"

"You're a hero," she says, shooting me a glance and then staring out at the city.

"I'm no hero."

"Well, it seemed to be what people wanted to hear these days. Gives people hope there's still something worthwhile in humanity."

"You gave them that."

She laughs, "I don't think so."

"I guess it's good practice for becoming a famous composer. You'll be talking to reporters all the time."

"Maybe," she says. Her eyes scan over me. "So, what's the deal with you? The doctors wouldn't tell me too much about you."

I shrug, "I got some bumps and bruises. Hearing isn't the

same, like you. And…I got a new leg."

"What?" she exclaims. "No. You're joking, right?"

I lean forward and roll up the ankle of my pants until she can see part of the metal rods. Her hands shoot to her face, covering her mouth as she gasps, "Oh, my god." She squints at my leg, and her eyes well up with tears. "I'm so sorry. This is all my fault. I can't believe you lost your leg. Oh my god, oh my god." She's starting to hyperventilate.

"Hey, listen," I say, trying to calm her down. "It's ok. I'm ok. This thing is pretty incredible, to be honest. Besides, now I can tell people I'm part robot."

The joke has the desired effect; she chuckles and regains her composure while I cover my leg.

"Does it hurt?" she asks.

"Some days are better than others, but it's not too bad."

She shakes her head. "I'm so sorry."

"It's ok."

There's an awkward silence as she processes my new leg and her role in my getting it.

"So, where have you been staying?" I ask, in hopes of distracting her from her thoughts. "I take it that has something to do with the new clothes."

Her expression changes as if she has something to tell me that she thinks I won't want to hear. She wipes the remaining tears with the back of her hand.

"After the journalist published the story, my photo was out and about for a while," she says. "A nice family found me, and… and I got adopted. I've just started living with them this week."

"Really? That's great," I say. "Isn't it?"

She shrugs and looks like she might cry again. She says, "I feel bad."

"About what?"

"You saved my life. I owe you everything. The fact that I'm even with these people is because of you. I don't know how to explain it." She pauses and picks at some chipping nail polish. "You've lost so much. You literally lost a part of yourself to keep my life going. And you didn't even really know me. And yet you still did it. It just doesn't feel right that I should get to have these things now."

I shift on the bench. "Can you look at me, Harper?" I wait until she does. "You don't owe me anything. I helped you because I could, so you could have exactly this. A life. A life that wasn't cut short because of something you had nothing to do with. If this family is nice and cares about you and will give you a good home, then that makes me happier than you can ever know." I smile. "This is all good, Harper. I'm happy for you. And if they ever give you any trouble, they'll have to answer to me."

She nods and smiles back. She doesn't say anything for a bit and watches the clouds drift overhead. Then she perks up as if she suddenly remembered something. She opens her purse and says, "I got you something." In her hand is a cardboard box that's a little bigger than a harmonica. "It's not much and is nothing compared to what you should get, for you know, saving my life, but it's all I could afford. I bought it with my own money."

"You didn't have to do that."

She hands me the box, and I remove the top. Inside is a wood-handled folding straight razor. I pick it up and open the steel blade.

"I remember you saying you needed to shave," she says. "The guy at the store told me this would last a lifetime and didn't require much maintenance. They even etched your initials into the handle too. Do you like it?"

It's one of the most thoughtful gifts I've ever received. And the fact that she used her own money simultaneously breaks and fills my heart. "I love it," I whisper. "Thank you."

"Good," she says, pleased. She fidgets slightly in the quiet. "Well, I should get going. My parents...the people who...my adopted family, are downstairs waiting for me."

"Ok," I say. "Thank you for the razor, and thank you for the visit."

We stand, and she hugs me again.

"Do you think, whenever you get out of here, that I could come to check in on you from time to time? If that's weird, I totally understand."

"I'd like that very much," I say. "I don't have a phone right now, but any messages you send, I'll see them when I'm up and running again."

She jots down her number on the box of the straight razor, and she inputs mine into her phone.

"I've been trying this thing where I don't say goodbye anymore as that feels too permanent," she says. "So, I'll see you soon."

I smile. "I'll see you soon."

I watch her until she gets to the door of the hospital. She stops and waves, then she's gone. I slide the straight razor into my pocket, walk to the rail, and rest my forearms on it. In the tree next to me, two robins land on a branch. I gaze over the battered and bruised city. Thankful that Harper's alive. Thankful that I'm alive. The thought brings a smile to my face as I listen to the robins sing.

DEDICATION

To all of my friends and family that helped make this book a reality either directly or indirectly. Your time and encouragement have meant the world to me. Special thanks to Teresa Pelham for her continued help with proofing.

MATT DURAND

11.1.2022